BEHIND THE SCHEME

C.E. KINGSLEY

CONTENTS

AUTHORS NOTE

Trigger warnings

THIS BOOK CONTAINS strong subject matter that may not be suitable for all readers. The topics in this book involve:

Abuse
Graphic rape
Kidnapping
Torture
Violence.
Reader discretion is advised.

PROLOGUE

Clink. Clink. Clink.

Pain travels throughout my body. What happened? Groaning, I open my eyes but am met with darkness. Chills run through my body as I feel my surroundings. I'm laying down on a cold cement floor, chains wrapped around my wrists.

Clink. Clink. Clink.

It sounds so far away. Metal against metal. Why would someone be making that sound?

"Wh-who's there?" I timidly say.

Heart rate rising, I push myself off the ground to sit up. Feeling restricted, I look down to see metal cuffs that are tight and digging into my wrists.

Clink. Clink. Clink.

The sound gets closer. Scooching backwards, I hit a cement wall.

Clink. Clink. Clink.

Flinching, I scurry away to my left. The chains pull against my wrists, pulling me back in the direction I'm trying so hard to get away from.

"Look who decided to wake up," a deep voice breaks the silence.

Shaking, I try to move away from the voice. I pull my arms to my chest when I feel tugging on the chain.

The man yanks the chain. I fly forward, hitting my head on metal bars and breaking my skin. Groaning, I slowly sit back up. Blood oozes out of the cut on my head, rolling down my face. Leaning my head against the bars, I take in a shaky breath. Pain radiates all over my head.

"We are going to have so much fun with you," the guy whispers in my ear.

Flinching, I move my body away from the bars. My head spins from the sudden movements. Nausea bubbles up and I swallow it back down.

I hear his footsteps fade as he walks away. "Franco, go tell the boss the bitch is awake."

The footsteps fade into the distance as I'm startled by a chair scraping against the floor next to me. How many other people are here with him? What do they want with me?

Keys rattle as I hear him unlocking the door. "Do you know what we do to bitches who owe us?"

What do I owe them? I only know the people in the motorcycle club, and I haven't heard them say anything about owing people. Not that they tell me much, but I do overhear the occasional detail that I shouldn't.

Hands grip my chin. "They get used, abused, and sold."

Thrashing around, I try to get my chin out of his hold. Gripping tighter, I can feel his fingernails dig into me. He breaks my skin and I hiss from the pain.

Stinging radiates across my face as it whips to my right side. "You'll get used by all of us first. Abused by all of us. And when we're done with you, we'll sell you to be used and abused all over again. That will be your life. Your body will never be the same."

Clenching my jaw, I try to calm my breathing down. Before I can take a breath in, knuckles connect with my cheek, sending my face to the left. Grunting in pain, sobs make their way out of my mouth. My face is sore and aching on both sides.

"One hit to the temple, and you're out for a couple of hours. Anyone can do anything to you, then."

Crying, I try to move my body away from the man. I don't want them to hurt me anymore.

Chuckling, he yanks my chain towards him, sending me flying. "You can't get away from us. You're our bitch, now."

Pain shoots across my head, my vision swimming. I roll over to my right side, my head hitting the ground, knocking me out.

CHAPTER ONE

MARCY

PLEASE READ AUTHORS NOTE FOR TRIGGER WARNINGS IF YOU HAVEN'T!

ONE DAY EARLIER

"Marcy! Get your ass down here so we can leave!" Noah yells at me.

Noah is the president's son of the motorcycle club, Hell's Reaper. He is two years older than me, making him nineteen, but we are best friends. Noah was living with his grandparents until I was five and he was seven. That's when I met him. As time went on, we grew closer and closer. My mom says that he took a liking to me and told his parents he wanted to stay at the club from now on.

I have had a small crush on him for years but didn't want to ruin our friendship by saying something. Gears has told me that I should tell Noah because he feels the same way, but I'm scared to do it. What if he rejects me? Then our friendship is ruined.

"Marcy!" Noah yells, banging on my door.

I groan and roll out of bed. The school year is starting tomorrow, and Noah wants to go out and get a couple of things. I don't want to go back to school and would rather be homeschooled, but both of my parents work full time and don't have time to homeschool me. I don't like being around people I don't know very well and the whole club knows that.

Noah makes it better by sticking to my side most of the time, but when we don't have classes together, I feel very uncomfortable and alone. Noah wanted me to skip a grade or for him to get held back one year, but our parents did not like that idea. They wanted us to learn how to be independent and not rely on each other for everything.

I don't think Noah relies on me as much as I rely on him. He helps calm me down when I get overwhelmed. He walks me to every class and gives me a hug. He shields me from the world and makes me feel comfortable around him.

"I'm coming in!" Noah says.

I watch the handle turn and I run to my closet, shutting the door. I quickly find the clothes I had laid out the night before and slip them on before I open my closet door. The first thing I see is Noah smiling and sitting on my bed.

"I should have said I was coming in earlier," Noah chuckles.

Giving him a glare, I walk up to him. He opens his arms out and I walk into his arms, giving him a hug. Even when Noah is sitting down, I am able to hug him while I am standing. He towers over me at six feet, but then again, I am really short, so most everyone does.

Feeling his arms wrap around me, I snuggle into his body. He gives some of the best hugs, not as good as my dad's, but a close second.

"Are you ready to go out and get a couple of things for school?" he asks, while rubbing my back.

"Yeah." I let out a sigh and pull away.

He gives me a small smile and stands up from my bed. He holds his big hand out and I place my small one in his. It feels so right to have my hands in his. I've wanted to verbalize that it feels right, but the fear consumes me every time I try.

"What are you thinking?" he asks, breaking me out of my thoughts.

"Nothing," I reply quickly.

"I don't believe you, but I'll leave it alone for now. Let's get going. I heard Butch is cooking lunch and I don't want to miss it."

I shoot up out of the bed and start to drag Noah down the stairs and to his truck. Butch's cooking is the best in the club. I wouldn't miss it for anything.

"Butch is cooking? Why didn't you say so. Hurry up," I rush out.

I hear Noah laugh. He knows I love Butch's food. Noah opens the door for me, and I climb into his truck. I watch him as he jogs around the truck and hops in on his side.

"I'm thinking of just going to Walmart to get school supplies. We don't need much." Noah turns on the car.

"I agree. I only need a couple notebooks, and some pens," I reply.

Connecting my phone to the aux, I start to play some Atreyu. Noah and I love listening to their band. My mom doesn't like the band at all, so I don't play it around her. Noah and I sing the whole way to Walmart.

"Come. Let's get this over with so we can head back," Noah grumbles out.

He doesn't like shopping at all, and I don't blame him. I don't enjoy it either. He knows how much I don't like it and planned this because he knew I would leave it to the last minute otherwise.

Noah grabs my hand and helps me out of the car before shutting my door. I give him a smile and we make our way into Walmart. Everyone knows who Noah is and gives him space. They aren't scared of him yet, but they are scared of his dad and what he will do. I don't blame them. Noah's dad can be scary when he wants to.

"You said only some notebooks and pens? How many notebooks and pens?" Noah squeezes my hand and I look into his eyes.

"Six notebooks and just two pens," I smile up at him.

Noah leads us to the school section and lets me pick out the notebooks and pens I want. He holds his hands out and I hand him my things. Noah is always the gentleman and carries my things. I act like it doesn't affect me, but I'm secretly swooning.

As Noah turns his attention to the notebooks to pick his out, I get a prickling sensation up the back of my neck that someone is watching me. Looking around, I can't see anyone near us. I shake off the feeling and move closer to Noah.

Once Noah has picked out his supplies, we make our way to the self-checkout line. I look over at Noah, making eye contact. We smile at each other.

We both step up to the register and I start to scan my things first. I reach for my wallet in my pocket but am met with emptiness. Looking up at Noah with wide eyes, I am met with a smile.

"Bear handed me this before I went to get you. He said you would most likely forget your wallet with the credit card in it," Noah explains, as he pays for my things.

"I'm sorry," I whisper.

I have a bad habit of forgetting things at the house when I go out. Being in Noah's presence makes me forget things.

"Hey, it's okay. No harm done. At this point, I think I should carry around your credit card so when we go out you don't even have to bring your wallet." Noah cracks a smile at the end.

"I actually was thinking of that. Any time we go out, I forget my wallet. When we get back to the club, I'll get my wallet and give you my credit card. Then I can start paying for my own food." I giggle towards the end.

"You know I don't mind paying for your food. It makes me feel like I am taking care of you."

Here Noah goes again with this type of talk. When he talks like this, he makes it seem as if he likes me. I can see what Gears is talking about now, but I always second guess myself a couple of seconds later.

"What's got you all silent?" Noah breaks me out of my thoughts.

"Nothing," I stutter out.

"I know you are lying, but you'll tell me when you want to."

I give him a small smile and we make our way to his truck. While we are walking to his truck, I feel the same feeling that someone is watching me. I stop walking and look all around me, but don't see anyone looking at us.

"Why'd you stop?" Noah asks.

"I feel like someone is staring at me. In the store, I also felt the same feeling. Someone is watching me." My voice drops towards the end.

I watch as Noah starts to look around the parking lot before turning back to me. He gives me a small smile.

"I don't see anyone looking at you. How about we go get hot chocolate? It's only ten in the morning and we will make it back to the club before lunch," Noah suggested.

I shake off the bad feeling when I feel the stare again. I look up at Noah and nod my head. Maybe getting hot chocolate with him will help keep my mind off of this feeling.

The hairs on my arms are standing up and my chest feels

tight with anxiety. I can feel my anxiety crawling up my chest and into my throat, making my breathing pick up.

"Well, come on," Noah opens the door for me. "Everything is going to be okay."

I hop into his truck and watch him walk around and get in on his side. I smile at Noah when he turns the car on, getting excited for some hot chocolate.

"You amaze me. Any mention of hot chocolate and you instantly cheer up and forget what's bothering you." Noah laughs.

"Because it's so good! You can't tell me you don't enjoy it just as much when we go! I always see the way you drink it slowly to savor the taste," I reply.

"True. It is good, but I don't drop everything at the mention of it."

"I don't drop everything!"

"If someone was dying, and another person mentioned getting hot chocolate, you would leave the dying person to get it."

I stare at Noah with my mouth open.

"I would not!" I raise my voice.

"Yes, you would. It's just who you are when it comes to hot chocolate. Hopefully, if I was the one dying, you would wait until after I'm dead to go drink some." He looks over at me for a split second.

I go silent at the mention of him dying. I hate when he brings up his dying. I don't think I could handle him dying on me. I wouldn't know what to do with myself.

"Why'd you go silent?" he asks, filling the silence.

"You know I hate it when you joke about your death," I whisper, looking out my window.

"Hey, I'm sorry." He grabs my hand.

Looking at him, I give him a small smile. Blinking several times, I try to get rid of the tears in my eyes.

"How about we just go back and hang out with Gears?" Noah suggests.

"Okay," I whisper.

Noah turns the truck around and heads back towards the compound. Even though I want to get hot chocolate, I think that seeing Gears and hanging out with both of them will do me some good.

We sit in silence as we make our way through the town. The compound isn't far away from town, so it doesn't take us long to get back. Parking the truck, Noah gets out and walks over to my side.

Opening the door, he holds his hand out for me. "I wonder if Gears is still working on that old Harley. Maybe he will let us help out."

Noah and I both love watching and helping out when we can. We have learned quite a bit from Gears.

Grabbing his hand, he helps me out of the car and closes the door. He wraps his arm around me as we make our way towards the garage.

"Look who finally decided to show up, and he brings my favorite person with him," Gears yells and winks at me.

Smiling, I walk over towards Gears and wrap my arms around his waist. Feeling his arms wrap around me, I melt into his body. I love his hugs.

"Did you tell him?" Gears asks.

Shaking my head, I unwrap my arms from around him. Maybe I'll tell him tonight.

Walking back over towards the bike, Gears picks up a wrench. "Where did you go this morning?"

"We went out to get supplies for school. Didn't want to take too long and miss out on Butch's food." Noah stands super close to me.

Wrapping his arm around me, I lean into his body. I could get used to this. Gears looks at me, wiggling his eyebrows. Blushing, I look away and around the garage, trying to find my mom.

"Where's my mom?" I ask, looking back at Gears.

"Your dad and mom went out for breakfast, but that's probably code word for they are going to fuck each other." Gears grimaces at the end.

"Didn't need to picture that."

Looking up, I catch Noah staring at me. Smiling, I continue to stare into his green eyes.

"Want to stay here or see if we can sneak into the kitchen to get food from Butch?" Noah squeezes my side.

"Sneak into the kitchen." I lean more into his body.

"I need to talk to Marcy for a second. She'll meet you outside the kitchen in a couple of minutes," Gears speaks up.

Looking at Gears, I let out a sigh. I know the conversation that is about to happen. We have had it several times already.

Noah lets go and cups my cheeks with his hands. "I'll see you in a couple of minutes."

Kissing my forehead, he walks out of the garage and into the main building. Looking back at Gears, I place my hand on my hip.

Gears pats the chair right next to him. "When are you going to tell him that you like him?"

Sitting down in the chair, I let out a breath. "I don't know. I'm afraid that if I do tell him, that he won't like me back and the friendship will be ruined."

Looking at me funny, Gears grabs my shoulders. "He likes you. The kiss to the forehead. Holding you tight against him."

"Okay, I'll tell him today."

"Good. That boy would do anything for you."

Staring at him in disbelief, I let out a scoff. Noah wouldn't do anything for me. There is always a limit.

"No, he wouldn't."

"Yes, he would. He has that look in his eyes. The same look Bear has for your mother. The 'I'll kill anyone for you' kind of look."

"Maybe."

Chuckling, he gives me a big smile. "You guys will make a cute couple."

Laughing, I wrap my arms around Gears. Letting go, I get up and walk towards the door.

"Are you going to the studio tomorrow morning?" Gears asks.

Turning around, I watch as he has a smile on his face.

"Yes, I am. Need me to relay a message to my teacher?"

My ballet teacher and he have a thing going on. She doesn't want to admit it, but ever since she has moved to this town, Gears has been following her like a lost puppy. They have been dating for a couple of years now. I wonder when Gears will make it official with her.

Ever since I was born, Gears has been someone I've gone to if I didn't want my parents to know.

"Nah, on second thought she wouldn't like that." Gears shakes his head.

Laughing, I walk through the doors and towards the kitchen. Spotting Noah outside the kitchen, I wrap my arms around his waist.

"How was your talk with Gears?" Noah wraps his arms around me.

"It was good." I look up and make eye contact with him.

Running his hands through my hair, he holds me closer to him. Maybe now would be a good time to tell him.

"Can I tell you something?" I mumble in his chest.

"You can tell me anything." He kisses the top of my head.

"I like you," I whisper.

Holding my breath, I wait for him to say something. Pulling away from me, he cups my cheeks with his hands.

"You want to know something?" he whispers back. "I like you too."

Smiling, he kisses my forehead and places my head back on his chest. Sighing, I snuggle into his chest.

"I was nervous to tell you. I thought you may not like me back and not want to be my friend after I told you," I mumble into his chest.

"Never. I've been thinking of how to tell you. I thought I had given some signals, but maybe I didn't." He holds me tight.

Before I have a chance to respond, Butch yells, "Finally! I've been waiting for years!"

Jumping, I pull away and look into the kitchen. Butch is staring right at us with a big, goofy smile. Blushing, I bury my face in Noah's chest.

Noah and Butch laugh at my action. If I had known Butch was watching, I wouldn't have told Noah. Looking back at Butch, he gives me a thumbs up.

"Alright! Come in the kitchen and grab some food." Butch gets back to working in the kitchen.

Noah grabs my hand and pulls me into the kitchen. Grabbing two plates, he fills both of them up and places one in front of me.

"Thank you." I smile.

Nodding, Noah and I dig into our food, making conversation now and then with Butch.

CHAPTER TWO

MARCY

"No! I told you to do grande jete, not pirouette," Antoinette yells at me. "Again!"

Taking a deep breath in, I close my eyes and relax my body. I've been practicing ballet since I was six years old. Antionette or as we call her, Annette, moved to Austin and opened a ballet studio. My mom immediately signed me up for classes.

Opening my eyes, I see Annette looking at me through the mirror. Jogging straight ahead, I leap in the air and spread my legs. Landing gracefully, I turn and look expectantly at Annette.

"Amazing!" She claps her hands.

Grinning, I walk over towards her. Hearing the door open, I stop my movements and look over to see Noah walking into the room.

"Ms. Moreau!" he yells.

Annette glares at Noah. "I told you to call me Antionette or Annette."

Smiling like crazy, he walks over to me. "I know, but someone has to get on your nerves."

"What do you need?"

"I am here to take Marcy to school, or we'll be late."

As she waves us away, Noah takes my hand and drags me out of the room.

"I'll see you tomorrow!" I wave to her as we walk out of the studio to Noah's truck...

He opens the door for me and places my bag in the back. "You can put your sweatpants on over your leotard on the way to school."

Nodding in agreement, I hop into the truck. I turn around in my seat to open my bag and grab my sweatpants. Quickly slipping them on, Noah gets into the truck and starts it.

"Are you nervous?" he asks, while putting the car in reverse.

As I put my seat belt on, I look over at Noah. "Yeah, I am. I don't know what I am going to do when you graduate."

Driving towards school, Noah grabs my hand with his free one. "You'll be okay. I'll be able to pick you up and drop you off. Maybe even sneak in for lunch."

Letting out a breath I didn't know I was holding; I watch the trees pass in a blur as we make our way towards the school. This will be my third year at this school, and it never gets easier.

Squeezing my hand with his, I look over at Noah. "Everything will be okay. If it gets too overwhelming, come find me. I've talked to some of the teachers, and they understand, or text me and I'll come up with an excuse to leave the room."

"Okay," I whisper.

Pulling into the parking lot, I take a deep breath in. Everyone stares at Noah's truck. They all know who it is and what MC he belongs to. Parking in the front row, Noah turns to me.

"Take a deep breath in with me." Noah takes a breath in.

Following his lead, I take a deep breath in. Watching his mouth, I exhale as he starts to. Looking into his eyes, I relax.

Smiling, he grabs my hands. "Ready to go in?"

Laughing, I unbuckle myself. "Not really, but I never will be."

Opening the car door, I hop out of the car and close the door. As we walk around, Noah has both of our backpacks on his shoulder. He wraps an arm around me as we walk into the school.

"Everyone is staring," I whisper, leaning into his body.

Holding me tighter, he kisses the top of my head. "They do this every year and every year we get through this."

"This time is different."

"Because we are a couple?"

Nodding my head, I look down at our feet as we make our way through the school. Noah stops walking and grabs my face with his hands, bringing my face up.

"Don't you ever look down at the ground again. I know it's uncomfortable, but we don't let it show. I am right here with you. We will get through this together," Noah firmly says.

As I nod my head, Noah lets go of my face. Wrapping his arms around me again as we make our way to our lockers.

"I'll walk you to every class. We also have lunch together." Noah opens my locker for me.

Picking up my history book, I turn towards Noah. "Does Audrey have lunch with us, too?"

Audrey is Annette's daughter, and she's also my friend. She is a year younger than I am. She normally practices with me in the morning, but Annette said she didn't sleep well last night so she will be practicing this afternoon.

"Yeah, she does. She said she'll meet us at our normal table." Noah closes my locker.

Turning right down the hall, we make our way toward my classroom. The whole way to the classroom we don't talk. Nerves start to bubble up in the pit of my stomach.

Stopping right in front of the room, I turn towards Noah. "I'm so nervous. I just want this day to be over with."

Pulling my bag off of his shoulder, he hands it to me. "You'll be okay. The day will be over before you know it, and then we can go home and relax."

Taking a deep breath, I glance inside the classroom. The room isn't full yet, but it will be soon.

"I'll see you after class." He kisses my forehead.

"See you," I mumble.

Chuckling at my face, he turns around and walks to his class. I wish we had the same classes this year. Closing my eyes, I take a deep breath in before I open them and walk into the classroom. Making my way towards the back of the classroom, I sit next to the window.

Noah taught me to sit in the back and next to the window. Teachers apparently leave kids alone when they sit there. It makes me calm knowing that the teacher won't call on me. I don't think I could handle that.

"Good morning class. This is US history. I am Ms. Nicole and I'll be your teacher for the year...," Ms. Nicole goes on.

Tuning her out, I look out the window at the trees. You can tell fall is coming since all the leaves have started changing color. It's my favorite season. For the rest of class, I stare out the window occasionally paying attention to the teacher while she talks.

* * *

He kisses my forehead as he grabs my hand, and we walk towards the lunchroom. "How were your first three classes of the day?"

Letting out a sigh, I look up at him. "I zoned out during the first two. The third one was art."

He gives me a disappointed look as he shakes his head. "You need to pay attention to your other classes. I know you love art, but history and English are important too."

"I know I do. I just don't like them. I want to be an artist, not an English or history teacher."

We et in line as Noah picks up two trays. He hands me one of them, and we walk forward.

"I know baby, but it's still important for everyday life. I'll help you study if you need it," he says, while picking up slices of pizza for us both.

Walking further down the line, Noah also grabs us fries. Every year, Noah and I eat school food for the first two weeks and then we bring our own. I don't know why, but it's become our tradition.

At the end of the line, I pay for my lunch and the cashier waves me along. While I wait for Noah to pay, I survey the lunchroom, spotting Audrey at our usual table.

"Come on, Audrey is waiting for us." Noah puts his hand on my back.

People stare at us as we walk toward our table. I focus on Audrey to distract myself from the stares. I place my tray down on the table.

"My mom will kill you for eating that stuff." Audrey takes a bite of her sandwich.

Audrey is a tall girl. She has wavy brunette hair that lands in the middle of her back. She's thin, but if you mess with her, you'll land on your ass. She has muscles, but you wouldn't be able to tell with what she normally wears. Baggy clothes to hide her figure.

"What she doesn't know won't hurt her." I eat a fry.

Noah laughs. "It'll only be for a week or two."

"A week or two too long," she mumbles.

Shaking my head, I take a bite of my pizza. It's not the best, but I am so hungry I don't care about the taste.

"What are you doing this afternoon?" Audrey asks.

"Probably hanging out in the garage." I take a sip of my drink.

"I can come over when my practice is finished. Hopefully, my mom won't make me practice for five hours."

"That's why you should practice in the morning. She can't keep you for an extra three hours since we have to be at school."

Groaning, she sits back in her seat. "I know. I won't make that mistake again. I regret not practicing this morning."

Sitting in silence, I finish off my pizza and fries. Lunch is almost over. I'm dreading going back to class.

"I'll throw that away for you." Noah picks up my tray.

Smiling, I watch as he throws away our trash and places the tray in the basket. Walking back over, Noah sees me smiling and returns it with one of his own.

"You guys are so cute," Audrey gushes.

Blushing, I lean into Noah's arms when he sits down. Not even a minute later, the bell signaling the end of lunch is ringing. I let out a sigh at the sound.

"Come on, let's get you to class," Noah says as he stands up.

Grabbing my hands, he helps me up. I grab my bag and sling it around my back, starting to walk toward my next class.

"I wish I could be homeschooled," I whisper, leaning into Noah while we walk.

"I know, but it's good for you to go to school in person. Interact with kids our own age." He kisses my temple.

Stopping in front of my classroom, I turn towards Noah. "I'll see you after this class."

"Actually, I'll see you at the end of the day. I know I promised that I would take you to every class, but my English teacher needs help with something on the first day and I couldn't say no." He smiles.

"That's okay. I understand. I'll see you later."

He kisses my forehead as he walks towards his class. Watching him walk away, I take a breath in. Every time he leaves, I feel a longing to be back with him. He's been with me since I was little and leaving each other never gets easier. His tall, muscular frame towers over most girls as he walks towards his class.

Turning around, I walk into my class. Sitting down in my chair, I drone it out as the teacher starts to talk.

* * *

Walking out of school, I look around for my parents. Noah has soccer practice after school today, so my parents pick me up. On days he doesn't have practice, he drives us home.

As I spot my parents, I make my way towards them. I make it halfway across the parking lot before a van comes to a stop in front of me. I go to walk around the back of the van, but suddenly the door slides open and two people in masks jump out.

They make like they are going to grab me, so I scream, and I run.

"Dad! Mom!" I frantically scream.

I suddenly feel arms wrap around my body. I thrash and scream for help while trying to break their hold. When they jerk me backwards, I stumble and lose my footing.

"Marcy! Where are you?" I hear my mom yell.

"Mom!" I scream.

The man drags me closer to the van. I keep thrashing but his hands keep tightening painfully around my arms.

Whipping my head to my right, I see my mom and dad running toward me. "Marcy!"

I feel myself being thrown into the van, hitting the floor of the van really hard, making me cry out in pain. Sitting up straight, I push myself up and try to jump out of the van.

"Mom!" I cry out as one of the masked men holds me in a painful grip.

One of the masked men slams the door, cutting off the view of my parents running towards me. Crying out in fear, I flail my arms, hitting one of the masked men. A hand connects to the side of my face immediately. The pain radiates across my face.

"Don't fucking hit me, bitch," the masked man yells at me.

Flinching, I scootch back and accidentally bump the legs of another masked man. He wraps his hand around the front of my neck and squeezes.

"Such a pretty bitch," the guy whispers in my ear.

Gasping for air, I claw viciously at his arms, digging deep with my nails as I draw blood. He lets go of my neck and punches me in the side of my face. I scream as pain radiates across my jaw, tears streaming down my face.

The other masked man grabs my hands and binds them together with rope. As the other man ties my feet together.

"We are going to have so much fun with you. I can't wait until the boss lets us have our turn with you." The masked man I scratched pulls my hair.

Dull pain appears the longer the guy pulls at my hair. I groan in pain as tears pool in my eyes.

"Please. I'll do anything. Let me go," I beg.

"Be quiet!" the driver yells.

"Please! I beg you. I'll do anything!" I sob.

"Shut the bitch up!" The van speeds up.

Looking around the van, I watch as one of the masked men moves closer to me. Before I can protest, pain explodes across my temple. In slow motion, my body sags sideways onto the van floor. The last thing I feel are unfamiliar hands all over me as I pass out.

CHAPTER THREE

MARCY

Sharp pain spreads across my head. Groaning, I try to move my hands to my head but can't. I open my eyes and am met with the van floor. My hands and feet are still bound together by the rope.

"Apparently, you didn't punch her hard enough. The bitch is awake again," someone grumbles.

Turning my head to the side, I am met with two pairs of eyes on me, one green and the other brown. Smiling wickedly at me, the one with the green eyes opens a bag and pulls out a white cloth. I stare at him with wide eyes.

Nothing ever good comes out of a white cloth. Every movie shows that once it goes over your mouth and nose, you pass out. There's no getting away from this, and my body and mind know it.

"Please, no," I whimper.

I don't want to be drugged.

"This should knock her out until we get back to the compound." The guy brings the cloth towards me.

Squirming, I try to put as much distance between myself and him as I can. I don't notice the brown-eyed man is beside me until it's too late and the pain from his fist hitting me starts radiating across my abdomen. Wheezing, a pair of arms wrap around my stomach as the cloth is placed against my mouth and nose. I hold my breath, not wanting to breathe in the chemicals.

"Breath in, bitch, or I'll hit you again, so you do," the guy holding the cloth says.

I shake my head while my lungs scream at me for air. I try my hardest to not breathe in.

"Hit her," he grumbles.

Arms disappear and grab mine, bringing them off my body. Pain rips across my stomach, making me grunt as he punches me repeatedly in the stomach. I am forced to take a gasping breath and I inhale the chemicals.

Instantly I feel them working. My vision goes blurry, and my body feels heavy. Panicking, I blink several times, trying to stay awake, but it doesn't work.

"Nighty night." The guys chuckle.

* * *

CLINK. Clink. Clink.

Pain travels throughout my body. What happened? Groaning, I open my eyes but am met with darkness. Chills run through my body as I feel my surroundings. I'm laying down on a cold cement floor, chains wrapped around my wrists.

Clink. Clink. Clink.

It sounds so far away. Metal against metal. Why would someone be making that sound?

"Wh-who's there?" I timidly say.

Heart rate rising, I push myself off the ground to sit up. Feeling metal around my wrists, I look down to see metal cuffs. They are tight and digging into my wrists.

Clink. Clink. Clink.

The sound gets closer. Scooching backwards, my back hits the cement wall.

Clink. Clink. Clink.

Flinching, I scurry away to my left. The chains pull against my wrists, pulling me back in the direction I'm trying so hard to get away from.

"Look who decided to wake up," a deep voice breaks the silence.

Shaking, I try to move away from the voice. Feeling a slight tug on the chain, I pull my arms to my body.

Someone yanks the chain, and I fly forward, hitting my head on some metal bars. Groaning, I slowly sit back up. Blood oozes out of the cut on my head, rolling down my face. Leaning my head against the bars, I take in a shaky breath. Pain radiates all over my head.

"We are going to have so much fun with you," the guy whispers in my ear.

Flinching, I move my body away from the bars. My head spins from the fast movements. Nausea bubbles and I try so hard not to throw up.

Footsteps walk away from me. "Franco, go tell the boss the bitch is awake."

I hear a chair scrape against the floor as footsteps walk further away from us. How many other people are here with him? What do they want with me?

Keys rattle as I hear the guy unlocking the door. "Do you know what we do to bitches who owe us?"

What do I owe them? I only know the people in the MC, and I haven't heard them say anything about owing people. Not that they tell me much, but I hear some things.

Hands grip my chin. "They get used, abused, and sold."

Thrashing around, I try to get my chin out of his hold. Gripping tighter, I can feel his fingernails dig into my skin. He breaks my skin and I hiss from the pain.

Stinging radiates across my face as it whips to my right side. "You'll get used by all of us first. Abused by all of us. Then we'll sell your body to other people, and they will use and abuse you."

Clenching my jaw, I try to calm my breathing down. Before I can take a breath in, knuckles connect with my cheek, sending my face to the left. Grunting in pain, sobs make their way out of my mouth. My face is sore and aching on both sides.

"One hit to the temple, and you're out for a couple of hours. Anyone can do anything to you, then."

Crying, I try to move my body away from the man. I don't want them to hurt me.

Chuckling, he yanks my chain forward, sending me flying. "You can't get away from this. You're our bitch, now."

Pain radiates across my head, my vision swarming. Feeling my body fall to the right, my head hits the ground, knocking me out.

* * *

GASPING FOR BREATH, I open my eyes and look around. It's lighter than the last time I was awake. I think I've gone in and out of consciousness a few times since the man hit me. I was never awake longer than a few of seconds. I don't know if they injected me with something to make me so groggy or if it was just the multiple hits to my head.

Turning to the right, I can faintly see past the bars. I see that it's a cell like mine, but empty. Looking over to my left, I am met with a pair of frightened eyes that belong to a young girl sitting in the corner.

The sight of her is startling. I scramble over to the further corner away from her in my cell. Trying to take in my surroundings, I start looking around for a way out of here. I notice the girl isn't chained to the wall like I am. Taking a breath in; I make eye contact with her, waiting for her to make her move.

She moves her hand, forming an O, K, and pointing at me. Tilting my head, I continue to stare at her. Registering what she says, my eyes start to water. I am not okay. I don't know how she is not crying or trying to get out.

"I want to go home. We need to get out of here," I cry out.

Panic flashes in her eyes. Whimpers come out of her mouth as she shakes her head several times. Taking a deep breath in, silent tears stream down my face.

"When they come back, we can jump them and leave," I whisper, completely forgetting about the chains around my wrists.

She shakes her head vigorously. She slowly starts to crawl toward me. Moving forward, I am met with the sound of metal hitting metal. Cringing, I look down at my hands. Fucking chains.

Crying louder, my whole body shakes. I just want to go home. The girl stops crawling toward me, panic and worry cross her face.

The sound of footsteps echoes in our direction. The girl starts to move away from me as she shakes her head at me. Pointing to her eyes she waves her hand. What is she trying to say?

The door opens to our cell and a burly man walks in. Looking straight at me, his face morphs into anger. He stalks towards me, raising his hand. Pain travels across my face.

"Bitches aren't allowed to cry here!" the man yells in my face.

More tears stream down my face. My whole body is aching from the previous punches I got. Shaking, I continue to cry from all the aches and the man yelling at me.

"I said shut up, bitch!" He punches my face, sending me to the ground.

My face connects with the concrete. I scream in pain, as my whole body shakes I sob. I bite my lip as hard as I can to stop crying, but it doesn't work.

The guy takes several steps towards me. Lifting his right foot he kicks me repeatedly in the stomach. Excruciating pain travels around my stomach as the guy kicks me several times. Black spots appear in my vision. Groaning in pain, I bring my legs up to my stomach, trying to protect myself.

The guy grabs a fist full of my hair, bringing my head up as I'm looking at him. Locking eyes with him, I flinch. Cold, lifeless eyes stare back at me.

"Next time you cry and make a fucking noise, I will fucking beat you until you are on the brink of death." He spits on my face. "Understand?"

Nodding my head, the best I can, tears well up in my eyes. I blink several times, trying to get rid of them. I don't want to be hurt again.

"When I ask you a question, you fucking answer!" he yells in my face.

"Yes, sir," I whisper.

Not expecting him to let go of me, my head comes crashing down onto the concrete yet again. Biting the inside of my cheeks, I hold in a scream of pain. My vision goes in and out. I blink to try and clear it up.

I watch as the guy leaves the cell, locking the door on his way out. Bringing my legs to my chest, I hold myself. Silent tears stream down my face. I hide my face in my legs, so no one can see me crying. I don't want another beating. I haven't been here long, but I don't know how much more I can take.

Feeling hands on me, I thrash out of their hold. My eyes are wide open in panic. Looking at the girl, she stares at me with wide eyes, shocked at my little outburst.

Giving the girl a small smile, I bring my hands up to my face and wipe some tears away. The girl sits right next to me, putting her arm around me.

Tears fill my eyes from the comfort. I just want to go home. I don't want to be here anymore.

"What's your name?" the girl whispers.

I look up at the girl, shocked that she is speaking. She never once gave any indication that she could speak before.

"Marcy," I reply. "You?"

"Lilith, but you can call me Estella."

Leaning back into her touch, I close my eyes. Feeling my body relax and the adrenaline fade, the pain of my injuries bubbles to the surface. Pain radiates all over my body and I groan as it becomes unbearable.

"It'll be okay," Estella whispers.

Tears pool in my eyes. Everything won't be okay. My whole body aches. I've been kidnapped from my parents.

My heart aches thinking about my parents and Noah. Will I ever see them again? Tears stream down my face, thinking about them.

Blinking, I try to get rid of the tears, but they just keep coming. Closing my eyes tightly, I take in a shaky breath.

Exhaustion overcomes my body the more the adrenaline fades and I find it hard to stay awake. Maybe a little nap won't hurt me.

"I'll watch over you." Estella runs her hands through my hair.

CHAPTER FOUR

JILLIAN

"Can you believe it's been seventeen years since I had Marcy?" I turn towards Bear.

"And now we are going to have another one in six months. I can't wait," Bear replies.

"How did you know?" I ask.

I hadn't told Bear that I was pregnant yet. I didn't know how he was going to react to me being pregnant again after all this time. I also wanted to do something cute this time, since I didn't do that with Marcy. What he doesn't realize it that he is off by a month. Our new baby will be here in five months, not six months.

"Baby, I know you and your body. You have started to change some and as much as you try to hide morning sickness, you can't." He hugs me.

I let out a sigh. "You are mostly right, Bear, except our little one will be here in five months. I just didn't know how you were going to take it. Especially since Marcy is grown now. We haven't had a little one running around for a while. I had hoped to do something cute this time." I pout.

He looks shocked as he meets my eyes. "You're already four

months along?" Then he shrugs. "It's going to be okay. We will love this baby just as much as we love Marcy. You still can for the rest of the guys."

I nod my head and relax into his arms.

"Are you ready to go pick up Marcy?" Bear asks.

I let go and walk towards the door. Marcy is almost done with school and loves us picking her up. She isn't like most teenagers who don't want to do anything with their parents. She loves it when anyone from the club picks her up, including us.

Bear and I hop into the car and make our way toward the school. It is a small public high school that every kid in town goes to. It doesn't take us long to get there. We get out of the car and lean against it, waiting for Marcy to get out of school.

"Mom! Dad!" Marcy yells.

We both turn towards her and wave. Bear and I look at each other and smile.

"She looks just like you," Bear says. "A little mini you."

"Is that a bad thing?" I jokingly say.

"Not at all. You are the best thing that ever happened to me, and she is the second. I wouldn't trade anything for you guys," he says, looking at me.

"Dad! Mom!" Marcy yells, frantically.

Bear and I whip our heads around to Marcy but can't find her. We both push off the car and look around.

"Marcy! Where are you?" I turn my head to the right but can't find her.

"Mom!" I hear her yell again.

I turn towards the road and see someone holding Marcy in their arms. They are carrying her to a van.

"Marcy!" I yell, running towards her.

Bear runs alongside me, trying to catch the kidnappers. The person holding her sits in the van, pulling Marcy in with them.

"Mom!" she cries out as the door slams shut.

Bear and I continue to run towards the car, trying to get to it before they take off. Before Bear can reach the van, it speeds off.

"Marcy!" I cry out, watching the car drive away.

My knees hit the ground as a sob makes its way out of my mouth. Bear curses and runs towards me.

"Jillian, everything is going to be okay. We'll get her back." Bear picks me up off the ground.

I wrap my arms around Bear and hold him tight. Sobs shake my body as he holds me tight against him.

"Who would want to do this to my baby?" I cling onto Bear.

He runs his hands up and down my back. "I don't know, baby, but we'll find out."

Holding my head against his chest, I continue to cry. I take a deep breath in and start to hear people talking. Trying to pull my head away from his chest, Bear holds me tighter against him.

"Shhh, I've got you. It's just some kids from the school," he whispers into my ear.

Tensing up, I hold my breath. Why didn't any of them help Marcy when she was getting taken?

"Let's get you in the car. I am going to call Gunner and wait for Noah and Audrey." Bear picks me up and starts walking.

Clinging onto him, tears continue to fall down my face. I hear Bear open the car door and he sets me on one of the seats.

"You stay here while I make the call and wait for the kids." Bear kisses my forehead.

Bear goes to close the door, but I grab his arm and stop him.

"Please don't leave." Tears start appearing in my eyes again.

I don't want to be alone right now. I don't think I can handle it.

"Okay, baby. I'm right here." Bear brings me closer to him.

I lean my head against his chest, hunching my body over to get comfortable. Bear starts moving his arms, placing one on my back.

"Phantom? I need you to run a partial license plate number. It was for a black van. The first part of the license plate was B74G, and I couldn't get a look at the second part," Bear's voice turns cold.

I hate when he does this. He puts up a mask and gets all distant and cold. He means business when he is like this.

"My fucking daughter just got taken! Run the partial license plate and find out where the fucking van is," Bear barks out. "We'll be at the compound soon with Noah and Audrey."

Hanging up the phone, Bear lets out a sigh. My body has gone ridged again from his conversation. I hope Phantom can find the van.

"Everything is going to be okay. Phantom is excellent at his job. He'll find the van and our daughter," Bear mumbles into my hair.

Before I can say anything, loud footsteps can be heard.

"Bear! Jillian!" Two voices shout.

Pulling away from Bear, I look out the front windshield. Noah and Audrey are running towards us.

"What happened?" Noah asks.

"I'll tell you and everyone else when we get to the compound. I need you to have a clear head while you drive back. We'll be following you," Bear says.

Noah looks into the car, searching in the back part of the car. Realization crosses his face. Opening his mouth, Bear beats him to it.

"I don't want to fucking hear it right now. We need to get back to the compound," Bear commands.

Noah closes his mouth. Grabbing Audrey's arm, he guides her towards his car. Bear shuts my door and walks over, getting into the driver's side.

"You could have been nicer," I say sniffling.

"No. Noah needs to do what I say. This is a fucking serious

situation, and he was going to ask questions when I fucking told him to drive to the compound. I told him I would tell him when we get there," Bear grumbles.

Bear pulls out of the parking spot and follows Noah to the compound. We pull into the compound, and everyone is standing out front. All of them have worried looks on their faces.

Bear turns off the car and gets out, walking around to my side. Unbuckling myself with shaky hands, I try to open the door. Bear opens the door for me instead.

"Shhh. I've got you." He picks me up.

Setting me on the ground, he holds me close to him as we walk toward everyone. I try not to look at people because I know I will start crying all over again.

"Did Phantom find anything?" Bear asks.

Looking up, I make eye contact with Gears. Tears are noticeable in his eyes. My eyes start to water again seeing him about to cry.

"I can't do this," I whisper. "I just want my baby back."

Bear pulls me closer to him, kissing me on the forehead. "I know, baby. We will find her."

Bear picks me up, placing my legs on either side of him and my face in his neck. I sob as he holds me close to him.

He runs his hands up and down my back. "Shh, you are going to make yourself sick. You need to calm down. Think of the baby."

Taking a deep breath in, I snuggle into his arms. Tears continue to run down my face as he starts talking to the guys.

"Let's get everyone in the house and we'll talk there," Bear says.

I hear footsteps heading towards the house. Bear starts walking to the house. He continues to run his right hand up and down my back, trying to calm me down.

"I've got a chair for her," Gears says.

Bear places me down on the chair and walks toward the group of guys.

"Give us the short version of what happened," Gunner, the president, says.

Everyone sits down, their attention on Bear.

"Jillian and I went to pick up Marcy. A van pulled up and took her. We couldn't get to her in time." Bear slams his hand on the table.

"I have something on the van!" Phantom walks into the room.

Everyone's attention turns to him. I start to feel hope. Has he found my daughter?

Phantom gives me a sad smile. "The van is registered to a Marcus Smith. It's a rental car that a group of guys rented for the day."

"Did this Marcus Smith have a name for this group of men?" Gunner asks.

"He did, but all of them were fake names. He said the guys sounded Italian or Russian."

"How does he not know the difference between Italian and Russian?" Gears questions in disbelief. "Is he a fucking idiot?"

Phantom rubs the back of his neck. "He sounded high when I called him."

"Does he have a fucking camera system that got their faces?" Bear stands up from his seat.

"He does. I'm going to go check them out tomorrow." Phantom pours himself a drink.

"Check them tonight! My daughter just got taken!" Bear yells.

"Calm down. Did you not hear that the guy sounded high? He won't be of any use right now. Phantom will check first thing in the morning." Gunner grabs Bear's shoulders.

I take a shaky breath in. I'm not getting my daughter back tonight. It all comes crashing down. Holding my stomach, I take a breath in before letting out a sob.

"Shit," Bear whispers.

Bear pushes everyone out of the way and kneels right in front of me. "Are you okay? The baby?"

Shaking my head, I lean forward as I continue to cry. Bear places his hands on my cheeks, holding my face so I'm looking him in the eye. It's all blurry with the tears in my eyes, but I can see the worry in his eyes.

"Baby, talk to me. Is the baby okay? Are you okay?" Bear rubs my cheeks with his thumbs.

"I. Baby," I fumble over my words.

"Take a deep breath in. That's it. You are doing great, baby. Follow my breathing."

My breathing starts to calm down, but I am still crying. I don't think I will ever stop crying.

"That's it. Now, is the baby okay? Are you okay?" Bear softly asks me.

"The baby is fine," I mumble.

I am so tired. Crying takes everything out of you.

"That's good. Are you okay?" he whispers.

Shaking my head, no, more tears fall out of my eyes. Bear gives me a small smile and holds me close to him.

"We will find Marcy. I promise." He kisses my forehead.

Everyone sits in silence as Bear and I hug.

"What are we going to do in the meantime?" Noah asks calmly.

"Phantom is going to check cameras around the area. I don't fucking care if you have to do it illegally. He is going to find the van," Gunner says.

"What about everyone else?" Noah stands up from his chair.

"We are going to wait. We don't have anything to go off of, right now."

"No! I can't just sit here and do nothing!" Noah yells.

I watch as Gunner grabs Noah's shoulders, he tries to calm him down. It obviously doesn't work because Noah rips his shoulders from his dad's hands.

"Don't touch me!" he bites out.

"Calm down, we are currently tracking the car down. You need to think back to the past couple of days. Has anything happened that was out of the ordinary? Did you see anyone watching you guys when you went to get school stuff?" Gunner asks.

Noah pales as his dad stops speaking.

"What happened?" Gunner takes a step towards him.

Noah looks up at his dad, tears brimming his eyes. "The day we went out to get school supplies. She told me she felt eyes on her."

CHAPTER FIVE

NOAH

I should have fucking said something. Marcy told me several times that she felt like someone was watching her, and I did nothing. I told her no one was, when there obviously was.

Anger starts to bubble inside of me. How could I let this happen? I should have scouted everything out once she said she felt like someone was watching her. I should have taken it fucking seriously and not told her no one was.

Taking in a deep breath, I try to remain calm on the outside. My dad always told me to never show emotion so the other people couldn't play you.

"What do you mean she felt eyes on her?" Bear calmly asks.

His calmness is deceptive. I know he is livid. I'm the same way. Bear is the best at hiding his emotions around the club.

"When we went out to get school supplies. She said a couple of times that she felt eyes on her. I looked around but didn't see anything. I told her nothing would happen." I pace back and forth.

I start to get worried. Is she being treated right? Fuck. Of course she isn't. She was fucking kidnapped. Is she still alive?

For all I know, they could have kidnapped her, and she could have pissed them off.

"And you didn't fucking say anything? This all could have been fucking avoided!" Bear yells, his anger showing some.

"Bear!" Jillian says, snipping at him.

Bear glares at Jillian. Even with tears in her eyes, she holds her ground. She is used to Bear's outbursts.

"Don't you fucking dare yell at him. I bet he has a good reason for not telling us," Jillian says.

Everyone goes silent and stares at her. Jillian doesn't curse much, but when she does everyone knows she means it. Bear continues to stare at her but doesn't say anything.

Jillian turns to me, giving me a tiny smile. "It's okay. What happened?"

Looking down at my feet, I blink away the tears. "We walked out of the store, and she said she felt someone's eyes on her. I looked around but couldn't find anyone that was suspicious. I told her no one would want to take her because she is too sweet and has done nothing wrong."

Looking back up, Jillian gives me a small smile.

"I should have said something, but when we got here, I forgot. Things happened, and it was the last thing on my mind," I grumble out.

"What could have been on your mind that made you forget?" Gunner asks.

Nervously looking at Bear, I glance over at Gears and Butch. They are both giving me smiles because they know what happened. I didn't ask Bear for his blessing to date his daughter. Fuck. I'm dead.

"Marcy and I started dating," I mumble.

"What was that?" Gears stifles a laugh. "Say it a little louder."

Gears always finds a way to laugh in a serious situation. He loves making people uncomfortable and getting other people mad at them.

"Marcy and I started fucking dating, alright."

Glaring at Gears, I see Bear tense up out of the corner of my eye. Great, I'm about to get the beating of my life. It's an unspoken rule that we are supposed to ask to date someone's daughter before we ask the girl.

Bear takes a threatening step towards me, cracking his knuckles and his neck. Standing my ground, I square my shoulders and look directly into his eyes. People whistle around us, caught off guard by what I did. I'm not about to back down now. Marcy and I started dating and I won't take it back.

"Not now." Gunner steps in between us.

Bear lets out a deep breath. "We're fucking talking later, Noah."

Gulping, I nod my head. I would rather have him give me the talk and beating now rather than later. Right now, we need to go out and find Marcy.

"Phantom! Get back to work," Gunner shouts.

Phantom goes back to work, leaving us to figure this out. What are we going to do? There are no leads on who they are or where they are taking Marcy.

"We are going to sit and talk about everywhere you have been with Marcy the past couple of days," my dad says, sitting down.

Anger boils in me again. Just fucking sit here? I don't think so. Marcy is on her own, and I'm not about to sit around and do nothing.

"We are going to fucking sit around and make a list while Marcy is fucking out there?!" I yell.

"Yes, son, we are," my dad replies. "We don't want to get into any more trouble with the law than we already are! We're on thin ice!"

Glaring at him, I raise my hand. "No! I'm not going to just fucking sit here while she is out there scared for her life!"

"You will do as your dad says. We need to know everywhere you two have been so we can look at cameras and see if there are any people who stand out." Gears places his hand on my shoulder.

"No! If this was mom, you would be out there trying to find her! You can't tell me to fucking sit down and make a list," I yell, moving out of Gears' hold.

"This wouldn't have happened if it were your mother. I would have paid closer attention! I would have killed whoever was staring at her!" my dad yells right back at me.

Hurt fills me as my dad says that. He has no fucking right to say that to me. The hurt turns to anger.

"You don't think I would do the same thing? It was a fucking mistake that I didn't tell you guys. I know, but it doesn't mean I won't do the same. I fucking love her! I will do anything to get her back," I spit out. "Even if that means fucking killing everyone in my way to do it."

A hand is placed on my shoulder. I try to move my body to get out of their grip, but they tighten their hold on me. Looking over my shoulder, I realize that Bear is holding my shoulder.

"You're going to all the shops and places they've been tomorrow, correct?" Bear asks. "We don't want to get into any more trouble with the law right now. I understand my daughter is missing, but we don't want to get put in jail and not get her back."

"That's right. Things are closing right now, and no one will be there," Gunner says.

"Then I'm taking Noah to the gym. We both need to let off some steam."

Bear continues to hold my shoulder as he steers me towards the gym. Ripping my arm out of his hold, I glare at him.

"I know where the fucking gym is. I can walk by myself," I grumble out.

I'm not a fucking child and he is treating me like one. Does he want someone to hold his shoulder and lead him in the direction they want him to go?

"So angry," Bear snaps back.

Staring at Bear in disbelief. Yes, I'm fucking angry. Why isn't he?

"Because my fucking girlfriend that I love just got taken away from me. Kidnapped. Why aren't you fucking angry? She's your daughter," I raise my voice.

We walk into his section of the gym and Bear closes and locks the door.

"Oh, I'm fucking livid. I'm just good at hiding it." Bear throws boxing gloves at me.

Catching them, I put them on, mumbling under my breath the whole time.

"Right now, you need to let off some steam. You being this angry will do you no good when you are trying to think about where you two have been the past several days." Bear holds up pads in his hands.

Shaking his head, he throws the pads away before grabbing some more boxing gloves. Putting them on, he takes a step towards me. He puts his hands to his side, leaving his chest wide open.

"Come at me," he says, keeping his hands to his side.

Stepping forward, I bring my hands up to my face. You never leave your face unguarded even if the person says they aren't going to hit you. I learned the hard way when Bear and my dad were teaching me how to fight.

A smile appears on Bear's face as I keep myself guarded. Taking another step forward, I quickly move my right hand and punch Bear straight in the chest.

"That was pretty wimpy if you ask me," Bear taunts me.

Anger rises in me as he talks. I'll show him who's wimpy. It won't be me. I continue to punch him in his chest and torso, not giving him time to recuperate.

Bear moves his hand, pushing my shoulder back. Getting off balance, I fall onto my ass. Scowling up at Bear, I get up and stalk towards him. How dare he do that.

"I know you are mad, but even when you are mad, you need to have a level head. Pay attention to your surroundings," Bear comments.

"I don't need your fucking lessons," I roar, punching him in the face.

His face goes to the side. Feeling smug about hitting him in the face, I take a step back and look at him. I bet he didn't think I would hit him there.

Bear takes a deep breath in and pulls his shirt off. Cracking his neck, he makes direct eye contact with me. Standing my ground, I bring my hands up to my face to guard myself.

He takes several steps toward me and lifts his right arm. Blocking myself from that punch, it never comes down. His left arm punches me in the gut, taking my breath away.

Kneeling on the ground, I try to suck in air, but can't. I was not expecting that at all. Finally, taking a shaky breath in, Bear steps right in front of me.

"Stay fucking alert," he spits out.

Looking up at Bear, I watch as his hand comes down. Pain radiates across my face as it goes towards my left. Groaning, I open my jaw to see if it's broken.

Bear steps right next to me and leans in close to my ear.

"When we get my daughter back, you better treat her fucking right," he growls out.

Bear steps away from me. Getting up, I wipe my mouth on

my arm and take a step forward. Bear leaves his chest open for me to hit him again.

"I..." *punch* "will fucking..." *punch* "treat your..." *punch* "daughter right." I continue to punch his chest.

Does he think I won't treat her right? That's not how I was raised. You treat women with fucking respect and nothing less.

"Good," is all Bear responds with.

Anger bubbles in me. Why would he say that and then just say fucking good? I continue to punch his chest and torso, not feeling any better about myself.

How could I let this happen to her? How could I let her get taken and not know anything? I'm so angry at myself for letting this happen. I should have taken fucking better care of her, but I didn't.

Tears of frustration appear in my eyes. I should have been there for Marcy. I should have told people and kept her safe. Punching Bear again, I can feel them start to get sloppy.

Taking a deep breath in, I blink away the tears and look at Bear. He is waiting for me to continue letting my anger out. Red patches run across his chest and torso from all the places I've hit. I even got him a couple of times in the face.

I take a step forward and get ready to punch Bear, but I don't anticipate his foot shooting out. He trips me, catching me in his arms. Holding me against his body, I start to cry.

"That's it. It's okay. We are going to find Marcy," he says.

I try to get out of his hold, but Bear holds me tight against him. This is embarrassing. I shouldn't be crying in front of Bear. I shouldn't be crying at all. I should be out there looking for Marcy.

"No one will ever know about this. Just let it all out. It will help you think clearer when we leave." Bear holds me tight.

I continue to fight to get out of his hold, but he continues to hold me tight against him. Taking a deep breath, I go limp in his arms and let everything out. Why did I not take her seriously when she said she felt someone was watching her? Why didn't I tell anyone about it?

It's all my fault. None of this would have happened if I had taken her seriously.

CHAPTER SIX

MARCY

I wake up to the sound of yelling. Several voices fill the air, and I can feel my whole body jerking awake.

"Go get the two bitches!" a guy yells. "Boss wants them up and working!"

I blink and look around. I'm laying on the ground of the cell. My body is ridged from the yelling. I've never liked yelling in my life, and all these guards have done is yell since I was taken. Estella grabs my arm and yanks me up. She quickly pushes my shoulders back, earning a hiss from me.

My whole body is sore. I don't think there isn't a place on my body that the guards haven't hit. Estella grabs my face and tilts it down. Keeping my hands in front of me, Estella gets in the same position beside me but puts her hands behind her. I would follow her lead and put my hands behind my back, but they are still bound together with the chains.

The urge to go to the bathroom grows in me the longer I stand up. Oh no. There is no bathroom here, only a bucket. I didn't have to go before, but now I do. What am I going to do? Shifting slightly, I try to get in a comfortable position but can't. This isn't going to end well.

"Stay still," Estella whispers.

I whimper, trying my best to hold my pee in. My bladder is so full I think if I take a step forward, I will pee myself.

"I need to pee," I whisper back.

Before Estella can say anything, footsteps get closer to us. Both of our bodies grow tenser the closer they get. Maybe they will give us food or unlock my chains so I can go to the bathroom. Keys jingle as the person unlocks the door.

Trying to keep it together, I press my thighs together. Maybe I can hold it long enough to ask to go to the bathroom. I bend slightly forward to relieve the pressure on my bladder. Shoes stop right in front of me.

Hands grip my hair, pulling my face up. I'm met with a scarred face. Thick white scars are scattered all across this guy's face. Smiling at me, I see all of his rotten teeth. Shuddering, I try to pull away from his touch.

"Don't pull away from me, bitch." He grips my hair tighter.

I move my hands in between my legs, trying to stop myself from peeing myself. This doesn't go unnoticed by the guard. A wicked smile appears on his face. He looks back at the guards and laughs before turning back to me.

"Ah, does the little bitch need to pee?" he taunts me.

Nodding my head yes, I open my mouth to ask if I can use a bathroom, but don't when the guard gives me a look.

"Pee." He steps back.

Looking at him in shock, I shake my head. I can't pee right here.

"We aren't leaving until you pee. Not in the bucket. You get to pee while standing in your clothes. We may even take pity on you and give you a new pair of clothes." The guy laughs.

The other three guys laugh with him. Tears spring to my eyes. This is so embarrassing. Not able to hold it in any longer, I move my hands and feel myself start to pee.

I hang my head as the warm liquid glides down my leg and makes a puddle around my bare feet. The men laugh louder. My shoulders start to shake as I finish peeing.

"Boss won't be happy if she smells like piss all day," a gruff voice says.

"We'll take her out back and hose her down," the guy in front of me says.

I keep my head down as the man comes closer and unlocks the chains around my arms. I feel so defeated by what just happened. The guy grabs my arm and yanks me forward.

"Follow me and don't think about running. There are guards everywhere," he says.

Following him out of the cell, we make our way to the right. Stairs lay ahead. The only noise heard are their shoes hitting the ground.

The guard opens the door, and the light shining through almost blinds me. I didn't realize how dark it was in the cell. I continue to follow the guard as we make our way around the building.

The guard behind me pushes me forward, making me fall to the ground. Before I can get up, cold water is being sprayed on me. Shuddering, I block my face from the water. I don't want to choke on it.

"Take your clothes off," the guard barks at me.

The water stops spraying me. I look over towards the guard, tears appearing in my eyes once again. This is so humiliating. I slowly start to take my clothes off, leaving my bra and underwear on.

"Underwear and bra, too." He laughs.

Hanging my head low, I unclasp my bra and pull down my underwear. I stand there completely bare, to the four men as they stare at me.

"The things I would do to you. Maybe the boss will let me have my way with you," the guy with the hose says.

Shuddering at the thought, I take a step back. I don't want them to have their way with me. One of the men steps closer to me, grabbing my breast really hard.

"I'll make sure when it's my turn that you won't be able to walk for a week. I'll make sure you bleed and beg for me to stop. You'll wish you were dead when I have my turn with you," he whispers in my ear.

Tears slide down my face as he continues his assault on me. All the fight has left me right now. There is nothing I can do. Four males against one girl. They'll tear me apart.

"Let her go. Boss wants her with no new bruises, cuts, and untouched," another guy says. "She's already banged up pretty bad. You touch her again, you'll be answering to the boss."

The man lets me go and steps back. My shoulders sag when he leaves. I feel so dirty.

"Boss won't notice if she has a couple more bruises. She's already covered in them," the guard says.

"Boss wants her to be able to move without hurting, too much, today. You know how he gets if they can't move fast enough," the guy retorts back.

"Follow me," he barks out.

I wrap my arms around myself as I follow him towards the big building. There must be five stories. We walk past more guards, all of them staring at me. I want to be buried six feet under, away from their prying eyes.

We step into the building, everything white and black. Clothes are thrown at me, hitting me in the face.

"Put those on," a guard grumbles.

Quickly putting them on, they stick to my body. Wet patches seep through the clothes. My hair is still wet, and I do my best to keep it on my shirt, so I don't leave water droplets.

Once the guard seems satisfied, he starts to walk towards a room. I follow after him, not wanting to meet his wrath. Estella stands there, hands behind her back, and her head down. I walk right next to her and imitate how she is standing.

"You two will be sticking together. You'll be cleaning every bathroom in this building. I want them spotless." A man steps in front of us.

Nodding our heads, we get handed supplies.

"Estella knows where to go," he grumbles.

Estella bows and starts to walk towards the door. Quickly bowing, I speed walk to try and catch up with Estella. For someone so small, she is very fast. Estella makes her way up the stairs.

I keep my head down as we continue our trek up the stairs. By the time we get to the top, I am out of breath.

"Hurry," she whispers.

Picking my head up slightly, I watch as a guard is walking down the hallway. Putting my head back down, I follow Estella into the bathroom.

"You can look up," she whispers.

Looking up, I take in everything. It's all white and spotless. I had taken little peeks around the house when we were walking, and it was the same. Everything is super clean. It's like no one lives in this house.

"You get started on the tub while I do the toilet and sink," she says.

Grabbing the soap and a scrubber, I walk over towards the bathtub. Pulling the curtain away, I look down. Not a speck of dirt can be found. Sighing, I turn on the shower to get the bottom wet before I squirt soap.

Getting down on my knees, I grab the scrubber and start to scrub. It really doesn't need to be cleaned, but I do it anyway.

Everything is so pristine and clean already. I wonder if the person who owns this house is a germaphobe.

Out of the corner of my eye, I can see Estella keeping a watchful eye on me. She probably doesn't want me to do anything out of order.

Sighing, I continue to scrub the bottom of the tub. Why are we cleaning this when we should be coming up with a plan to get out of here? Standing up, I throw the scrubby in the tub and turn towards Estella. Her eyes are wide as she stares at me.

"I'm leaving. We need to find out how to leave and get out of here!" I whisper yell.

Her eyes panic, and she holds my arm in place. Yanking my arm out of her hold, I step closer to the door.

"You can stay here if you want, but I am finding a way out!" I say.

Turning around, I walk over to the door and peek out. No guards in sight. Interesting. Every place we've been today there has always been a guard close by. Maybe they thought that we would be good by ourselves.

Sneaking out of the bathroom, I turn to my right. I remember walking up the stairs over here. Maybe the front door or any door leading outside will be on the first floor. Spotting the staircase, hope fills within me. One step closer to freedom. Now, all I have to do is go down and find a door leading outside.

Taking a breath in, I take another step closer to the stairs. Turning my head, I make sure no one is behind me, but I am met with a pair of eyes.

"What do you think you are doing?" the male barks out.

Stepping back, I try to turn and dash down the stairs. Not being quick enough, I feel the guy push my back, sending me flying forward.

Screaming, I cover my head as I tumble down the stairs. I hit my arms, back, and legs as I fall down the stairs. Not able to stop myself, I tense my body even more. It feels like the stairs go on forever.

Landing on the bottom with a thud, I take a sharp breath in. Everything hurts more than it did before. I feel like everything is broken and I can't move. I pull my arms away from my face and open my eyes.

Black shiny shoes step right in front of me as I open my eyes. Looking up, I'm met with a tall, huge man with an angry face. Fuck.

CHAPTER SEVEN

MARCY

Staring at the intimidating man, I take in a shaky breath.

"Did I say you could look into my fucking eyes?" his gruff voice fills the silence.

Looking down at his feet, I keep silent in my position. All I want to do is lay down and rest, but this man has an aurora of power. The way people don't look him in the eyes lets me know that he is important.

"Stand up!" he raises his voice.

I ignore the protest of my body and stand up quickly. Keeping my head down, I place my hands behind my back like Estella did earlier. The man takes a step closer to me.

"Did they tell you who I was?" he asks.

I shake my head no.

"Fucking answer me with words!" he yells.

"No, sir," I shakily say.

He steps to the side of me. I can feel his eyes looking over my body. My clothes are still a little damp and clinging to my skin.

"I'm Lorenzo Rossi." He grabs a piece of my hair and moves closer to my ear. "Italian mafia don."

Dread fills me. I've heard some of the guys in Hells Reaper talk about the mafia. They try to stay clear of them. They are ruthless and won't stop at anything to get what they want. Why would the Italian Mafia be in Colorado?

"You must be wondering why we are in the states and not back in Italy," Lorenzo says, walking behind me.

Lorenzo grabs my ass, making me squeal and move away from him.

"Did I say you could move?" He grabs my ass again.

"N-no," I stutter.

"You belong to me now." He lets go of my ass.

Taking a shaky breath in, I watch his figure walk back in front of me.

"Now, we came to the United States just for you." He twirls a piece of my hair.

Why me? I've never done anything to get the Italian mafia's attention.

"Ah, I see your facial expression. Ask your question," he says.

"W-why me?" I whisper.

He grabs my shoulder really hard. "In due time, I will tell you that, but you don't need to know right now."

Lorenzo lets go of my shoulder, and I let out a little sigh in relief. His grip was strong and pressed on one of my bruises. I know I will have bruises in the shape of his hands on my shoulder and ass.

The man behind him whispers something in Lorenzo's ear. Lorenzo goes rigid before he says something in Italian. I wish now that I took Italian instead of Spanish in high school. Maybe I would have been able to understand what they said to each other.

Lorenzo quickly turns towards me and grabs one of my boobs. Shrieking, I take a step back and cover my tits. His grip felt like nails getting hammered into my skin. Hard and painful. Lorenzo lets out a growl and grabs my arm, yanking me towards him. He starts walking in the opposite direction of the stairs.

Looking back, I make eye contact with Estella at the top of the stairs. You can see fear in her body stance and face. Estella quickly wipes away the tears rolling down her face. Getting yanked again, I stumble almost hitting Lorenzo. He opens a door to a room and pushes me inside.

I hit the ground, not prepared to be pushed. Landing really hard on my knees, I let out a whimper in pain. I don't think I am going to last a week here if they keep hitting me and pushing me places.

Lorenzo walks right in front of my kneeling form. He squats down and grabs my chin with his hand.

"Next time I touch you in front of people, you won't fight back. Do you understand?" His voice is cold.

Tears brim in my eyes. "Yes, sir."

Letting go of my chin, he stands back up. I go to stand up, but he stops me.

"Did I say you could move?" he says.

I get back onto my knees, keeping my head slightly down. I wanted to be able to see him move around the room but knew not to look him in the eyes.

"The things I get to do to you. Do you want to know them?" He walks around me.

I stay silent, not knowing how to answer. I don't want to know what he wants to do to me. Why would I want to know that?

"I'll have you in my bed, naked and tied up, so you can't go anywhere. A gag in your mouth so you can't call out for help." He continues to walk around me.

Silent tears roll down my face as he talks. I don't want any of this.

"Are you a masochist?" he asks.

"No," I whisper.

Pain radiates across my face. "No, sir. You're only allowed to call me sir after speaking."

"N-no, sir," I sob out.

"Hmm. I'll have to change that." He chuckles at the end.

My breath is taken from me. No. I don't do well with pain.

"I may take a whip. Your mom got whipped before. Such a pretty sight. I may have to do the same with you." He starts to walk around me again.

My mom? How does he know my mom? How does he know what happened to her? She doesn't talk about it much. She has given me bits and pieces of it, but she never wants to just talk about it, and I understand.

"I'm going to enjoy your body. Fucking you. Your sweet tight cunt and ass." He takes a piece of my hair.

It takes everything in me not to move. I don't want him touching me.

"Tell me, have you ever been fucked?" He grabs my chin.

"No," I whisper. "Sir."

I had almost forgotten to add sir to the end of it. I don't want to get hit again. Maybe if I continue to call him sir, he will go easy on me and not do anything.

"I'm going to enjoy taking your virginity. Pussy and ass. Oh, the joy it will bring me. Hearing you whimper for me to continue." He lets go of my jaw.

My body starts to tremble as he continues to talk. This is all a nightmare. I'll wake up soon and be back in Noah's arms. My parents will be right next to us.

"I'm going to have so much fun playing with your boobs. So perfect they can fit in my hands." He sits down on the bed.

He crosses his legs and looks at me. I continue to look at him through my peripherals, afraid to move. I want to run away and never return.

"I'll cover you in my cum. Not let you take a shower and walk around the house naked so everyone can see what I did to you." Amusement laces his voice.

I bet he would get a kick out of that, and I hope it never happens to me. Slightly moving my head, I get a clearer look at him. He is looking off into the distance. Maybe this is my time to escape. I bet I could make it to the door before he gets me.

As if he can sense my thoughts, he snaps his gaze to me. "I need to show you what happens when you disobey or try and run away."

He gets up from the chair and stalks towards me. I don't move, afraid that if I do, it will make my punishment worse. Maybe he'll punch me a couple of times and let me go back to my cell.

"I think I'm going to fuck that tight little pussy of yours," he whispers in my ear.

Jerking back, I try to stand up to get away from him. He will not rape me. I won't allow it. Lorenzo grabs my arm and pushes me towards the bed. Landing on my stomach, he puts a hand against the middle of my back and pushes down hard.

"You look so much like your mother. So beautiful," he says.

With his other hand, he starts to tug the leggings down my legs. They didn't give me any underwear earlier. Only leggings and a shirt. I wonder if they knew this was going to happen.

Struggling against his grip, I try to roll myself over. Lorenzo presses down more onto my back. I kick my legs back, hitting him really hard in the shin. The pressure on my back eases for a second and I take advantage of that.

Turning myself around, I start to move backwards away from him. He looks up at me and we make eye contact. Anger shows on his face and in his eyes. Before I can block it, he punches me in the face, immobilizing me for several seconds. Lorenzo takes advantage of that and grabs my hands.

Tying them to the bedpost, I wiggle around to get them undone. The rope digs into my wrists, making me whimper in pain. Lorenzo moves towards my legs.

Kicking my feet towards him, I try to hit him, but he's too fast. He grabs my right leg and ties the rope around it before tying it to the bedpost. The rope is too tight around my ankle, and I feel it going numb.

Lorenzo swiftly moves onto my left leg and does the same. I give up on my legs and focus on my wrists, trying to get them untied.

"You won't be able to untie them," he says, getting off the bed.

I continue to try and untie my hands. I watch as he starts to take his clothes off.

"Please, don't do this. I'll do anything you want if you don't do this," I beg.

He smiles wickedly at me. "Too late. You should have thought about that before you tried running away. Now, I get to play with you."

Fully naked, he crawls up the bed and hovers over me.

"Please don't," I say, sobbing now.

I try to wiggle around to get free or throw him off of me. My nightmare is coming true. He slaps my face, pain radiating across my cheek.

"Shut up and stop moving!" he yells.

He positions himself between my legs, ready to steal my virginity from me. Looking into my eyes, his lips spread into an evil grin.

"You're going to enjoy this," he says, ramming his dick into me.

I scream as he forces himself into me. It feels as if my body is being ripped in two as searing hot pain tears through my body. Tears run down my face as he continues pulling out and ramming back into me, not letting up in his assault.

"Please, stop," I scream in pain.

He doesn't stop, if anything my cries make him angrier. Making his thrusts faster and harder than before. He grunts as he gets closer to his release. Defeated, the fight leaves my body along with my will to live. I stop fighting, feeling numb and blank to what is happening to me.

"Stop," I whisper.

He ignores me and continues to thrust into me. It feels like sandpaper is moving in and out of me with each thrust. With his hand, he painfully presses down on my clit and starts to rub it, making me cum.

"Please," I beg, pain evident in my voice.

"Be a good little slut and shut up! Take my cock like I know you want to. Such a dirty whore," he grunts out.

My legs are starting to go numb. The ropes around my ankles and the position they are in isn't helping.

Lorenzo pulls out of me, and I let out a sigh. My vagina is throbbing in pain. He moves down to my legs and unties them. Grabbing my ankles, he pushes my knees up to my chest and rams back into me.

The pain becomes too much. My mind goes blank as he continues his assault. My hands feel as numb as my mind from the lack of blood flow. I gasp as he thrusts into me.

"You feel so good around my cock. Your tight virgin cunt," he grunts.

I lean my head to the right, trying to block everything out. Silent tears roll down my face with every thrust he gives me. I imagine my happy place, being with my family at the compound.

After what feels like forever, I feel myself slowly starting to lose consciousness. Lorenzo continues to thrust into me. He's untied my hands and feet, knowing that I can't do anything. He's changed positions several times, making it more painful for me.

With one last breath, I let the darkness take me.

CHAPTER EIGHT

MARCY

Hands run through my hair as I wake up. My whole body is aching, especially in between my legs. I stay still, trying not to move my aching body. Maybe if I continue to keep my eyes closed, I won't remember where I am. I'll pretend that my head is laying in Noah's lap, and he is running his hands through my hair.

Eventually, I open my eyes to see that I'm back in the cell. I shudder at the thought of Lorenzo continuing his assault after I passed out.

My head is laying on Estella's lap. I continue to stare at the bars of the cell, keeping my breathing even. Maybe I can keep my breathing even and just stay in this position. My body aches, but I know if I move it that it will hurt even more.

My mind drifts to what happened recently. I remember every detail. The searing pain of having my virginity stolen, the punches, slaps, and the numbness in my limbs from the ropes being too tight. I feel numb from everything. I don't know how to feel after everything that has happened. I don't know how to process it all, so I just turn off my emotions. I blink as I stare into the open cell.

Estella stops running her hands through my hair and wraps her arms around my body. It's an awkward position. Not knowing what to do, I continue to look at the bars surrounding us. There isn't much to do. She is showing me affection, but I don't feel anything.

I want to cry for everything that has happened to me, but my body won't let me. My emotions are locked away and I'm just a blank person. Soulless. No emotions to show anyone.

What is there to feel but pain and suffering? I've only been here for almost two days, and I've already been beaten and raped.

Footsteps come closer to our cell, keys clinking together as they open the door. The guard throws some bread and a bottle of water into the cell, and leaves.

Estella slowly helps me sit up. Once I'm situated, she stands up and grabs the food and water. She tears a piece of bread and hands it to me, but I don't take it.

Maybe if I don't eat, I'll just wither away and not have to be here anymore. I think dying from starvation would be better than dying from being beaten and raped.

Estella sits right next to me, breaks a piece of bread, and holds it to my mouth. I don't open my mouth at first, not wanting to eat, but Estella continues to hold the piece of bread in front of my mouth. I slowly open my mouth and Estella places it in.

As I chew the piece of bread, I realize that it doesn't taste like anything.

Estella and I sit for a while, her feeding me bread every once in a while and a sip of water here and there. The water bottle was half filled for the both of us to drink. You would think that they would take better care of us.

"You have to keep eating," Estella whispers to me.

I shake my head. I am so full right now. I don't think I can eat anymore.

"You need to keep strong." She presses another piece of bread to my mouth.

I open my mouth and feel her put it in. I don't feel like chewing anymore, but I make myself chew.

"Where were you before you got taken?" she asks.

"My high school," I hoarsely say.

"Right after you got let out?"

I nod my head. I wish I was more aware of my surroundings then. Maybe I could have gotten away.

"Me too, but when I was in second grade," she whispers, placing the water bottle on the ground.

"Sorry," I reply.

I don't know how to respond to that. How does someone respond to that?

"You have people that care for you. I bet they are looking for you right now." She grabs my hand in hers.

"Yeah, I hope they are." I lean my head on her shoulder.

I thought talking about them and where I came from would make me emotional, but I'm still numb. Or maybe I am in shock from everything that has happened. I do have hope that they are looking for me, but I don't know if I can face Noah after what happened last night.

Estella and I sit in silence for a while, just staring off into space. Estella has tried to make conversation, but I don't want to talk. She wanted to talk about what happened last night, but I don't want to even think about it.

"Whenever Mr. Rossi is around, act perfect. Don't anger him and whatever you do, please don't look into his eyes or flinch away from him," Estella pleads.

I never want to be around Mr. Rossi again.

"Please tell me you understand," she whispers.

"Yeah," I reply.

I completely understand. If I can avoid Mr. Rossi raping me again, then I will. I'll be so perfect. I won't give him a reason to rape me again.

We hear a door close loudly, and footsteps follow. I wonder what they want with us now. They already gave us food. Two guards and an unfamiliar man stop in front of the cell.

"Estella, go to the other corner!" one of the guards' yells.

The guard opens the door as Estella gets up. Estella walks over to the other side as the guard walks into the cell.

"Sit up straight, bitch. Doc is here to inject you, so you don't get pregnant," a guard says.

Staring up at the man who walks into the cell, my only guess is he is the doctor. He gives me a sympathetic look as he opens his bag. Getting out a needle and a bottle, he fills the needle up.

"This should help you not get pregnant while you are here. I may have to come back and give you a second dose depending on how long you last," doc softly speaks to me.

I blink, watching him sterilize the place he is going to inject the medicine into. I can hear his words, but they aren't registering in my head. The doctor gets closer to me and injects the needle into my skin.

"Don't react. I'm going to try and find a way to get you guys out of here," he whispers as he injects the medicine into me.

I continue to stare past the doctor, half listening to what he is saying.

"Alright, get up, doc. You know you aren't allowed to talk to the girls. The last guy got killed because he tried helping them. Move along!" a guard yells.

The doctor takes the needle out of my arm and packs everything up. He gives Estella and me one last look before leaving the cell and heading out of the building.

"Get up you two. You are in the kitchen today," the guard snaps at us.

Standing up, I walk over to Estella. We wait for the guard to move out of the way before we leave the cell. Keeping our heads bowed, we make our way up the stairs, out of the building, and into the other one.

Another guard starts walking in the direction of the kitchen as we follow him. I wonder what we will be doing in the kitchen. We could be cleaning, cooking, or prepping things.

"You two will be cooking, today. Make enough for ten people," the guard says as we step into the kitchen.

Looking at the kitchen, I take it all in. It's huge. There is plenty of counter space that has all different types of vegetables, meat, and fruits on it. The guard sits down in one of the chairs and gets on his phone.

Estella turns around and looks at the guard. "Sir?"

Looking up, the guard looks annoyed. "What."

"Are we allowed to speak while we work?"

He waves his hands toward us in a dismissive way. "Yes."

Estella pulls me towards the meat section. There are several different cuts of meat.

"What did the doctor say to you?" she whispers as she looks at the meat.

"I don't remember." I point to the New York strips.

And that's the truth. I remember him saying something to me, but I can't remember the words.

Estella picks up ten New York strips and walks over to the stove. Pans lay there, ready to be used.

"I was thinking New York strips with mashed potatoes, and some brussel sprouts," I tell Estella.

"That sounds good. Do you know how to cook meat?" she asks.

"Not really."

"That's okay. I kind of know how to. You can get working on the potatoes while I do the meat and brussel sprouts."

Nodding my head, I grab a sack of potatoes. Peelers and knives lay across the kitchen counter. I pick up the peeler and start to peel the potatoes.

"Did you cook before you came here?" Estella asks.

"Sometimes. I mostly helped with the side dishes if I ever did help. Butch was the main person who cooked. He taught me a couple of things, but he always handled the meat," I reply.

I gave away more than I would have liked, but I couldn't stop myself from speaking. It all just came out. Do I need to be careful of what I say around the guards? I probably should be.

I remember my dad and Gears telling me not to tell people much about the MC, since they didn't always do legal things. It was hard because I love the MC a lot, but I completely understand. I wouldn't want anything to happen to my family.

"That's cool. I've learned everything from here," she replies.

Nodding my head, I continue to peel the potatoes.

"How many should I peel?" I ask.

"I would do the whole bag," Estella says. "I've already got a pot of water boiling for you."

"Thanks," I reply.

I almost have the whole bag of potatoes ready.

"I'll help cut the potatoes. The meat is on the stove cooking and I don't have anything to do. The cleaning crew will be in here once we finish making and plating all the food," Estella says.

We work in tandem, and before I know it, everything is done and ready to plate. It was nice to be in the kitchen and cooking. It was nice to do something normal, today.

"I'll cut the meat and put it on the plate while you do the mashed potatoes and brussel sprouts," Estella says, cutting the steaks.

Grabbing the pan, I walk over to the ten plates. I don't know how much to put on the plates. Maybe a big spoon full. That's what Noah always ate. Deciding on that, I start to put a big spoon full of mashed potatoes on each plate. Once I'm done with that, I move onto the brussel sprouts.

"We're done," Estella says to the guard.

He looks up from his phone and stares at the plates.

"Let's go," he says, standing up.

He didn't look like he was paying much attention to us, but I know he was. All the guards are on high alert, even if they are on their phones or talking to someone. I've been watching them from my peripherals, and I can see their eyes moving from their phones to sneakily look around the room.

Estella and I follow the guard out of the kitchen to the guard standing by the entrance.

"Boss wants them back in their cell," he says.

The other guard nods and opens the door. We make our way outside and towards the other building. It is getting colder since the sun has started to go down.

We make our way back into the other building and to our cell. The guard locks the door before leaving us in silence.

I lay in my corner of the cell. Everything is crashing down on me as I take things in. I got raped. I've been beaten. Tears stream down my face. I place my hand over my mouth to keep myself quiet. I don't want the guards to come in and beat me.

I hear Estella moving around in the cell. My eyes feel heavy with every passing second. Closing my eyes, I feel myself drifting off to sleep.

CHAPTER NINE

MARCY

TWO MONTHS LATER

Two months have fully passed since I was taken away. A lot has changed around here. I've changed.

Estella had given me hope the third day that my family would come and rescue me. I had told her bits and pieces about them and how much they cared about me. As the days went by, I lost that hope.

It's been a nightmare here. Mr. Rossi had his way with me several times. Even if I didn't do anything wrong, he would have me delivered to his room so he could rape me again. He even has given some of his men chances to have their way with me.

I shudder at that thought. It's absolutely horrible and they show no mercy. Fear consumes me every time one of the guards walks in.

I've lost a ton of weight since being here. They feed us once a day and when they feel generous, it's twice. Estella and I have been put on kitchen duty. Mr. Rossi and the other men have loved when we cook, so it is now our job. We've tried sneaking food before, but it didn't work out so great.

A shudder runs through me as I think about that. It was a while ago, but it feels just like yesterday.

"Here, eat this little bit. They aren't looking," Estella whispers, handing me some food.

I quickly put it in my mouth and slowly chew. Closing my eyes, I savor the taste that spreads throughout my mouth.

"Hey! What are you eating?" a guard yells.

Looking over at him, my eyes go wide. The guard is stalking towards me, anger evident on his face.

"Who said you could eat the food here? Huh? Who gave you permission? This food isn't for a whore like you," he yells, slapping me across my right cheek.

Pain spreads across from the force he used. Before I could fully recover, he punched me in the stomach. I double over, gasping for breath.

Yanking my hair, he pulls my head up. "This will teach you not to steal food. Next time I'll fuck you."

Estella touches my shoulder, bringing me out of the memory. Never again did we try to sneak food to eat. After that, they added another guard to watch us.

They also don't want the boss to be poisoned, so they watch us like hawks. Having us only eat once a day makes us malnourished. If we are malnourished and always in pain from beatings, then we aren't as likely to fight back.

There are a couple of other girls that work for Mr. Rossi, but they look way better than us. I think they actually get paid to work here.

"They brought us food," Estella whispers.

"Not hungry," I mumble.

I've lost my appetite in the past couple of weeks. Every time

I say I'm not hungry, my stomach protests. I just feel dirty and don't want to continue to be here.

"You need to eat." Estella grabs my hands.

She places a piece of bread in my hand. I hold it, but don't eat it. The hunger pains have been gone for a while. It was hard in the beginning to only eat once a day, but as the guys continued to rape me and the longer I went without food, the easier it became.

"You need your strength. You've lost a lot of weight since you've been here," Estella says.

I turn my head towards her and hand her the piece of bread. She shoves the piece of bread back into my hand.

"No, you are going to eat it. I know you don't want to. I understand. I went through the same thing you are going through, but you need to continue to go on. You have people looking for you!" she says.

"No, I don't. It's been two months, and nothing has happened," I reply.

"Maybe they ran into complications, or they are coming up with a plan. You have to have hope."

"You didn't have hope when you got taken."

"I was different. I was so young, and my parents didn't care about me. You have a loving family and a boy who loves you."

Sighing, I close my eyes and lean my head against the wall. My parents, Noah, and all the guys in the club. I know deep down that they are looking for me, but it's so hard to have hope when it's been two months.

"Now, you are going to eat because you need your strength." She moves her hands, leaving the piece of bread in mine.

I stare down at the bread. I really don't have an appetite and I don't want to make myself sick by eating it.

"Little bites at a time," she whispers, taking the bread from my hand.

Tearing off a little piece, she places it in my hand. I shakily bring it up to my mouth and chew. I initially feel like throwing up, but after swallowing, it settles down.

"Good," she says, handing me another piece.

Estella and I continue like this for a while until all the bread is gone. My stomach feels so full that I'm worried if I move, I'll throw it up.

"Drink some of this," she hands me the water bottle.

Taking small sips of the water, I let out a sigh in content. The cold liquid coats my throat. I hand the water bottle back to Estella and watch her drink the rest of it. Oh, how I would love to be able to drink all of it, but I know Estella needs water. I can't be selfish.

"Rest now. I don't know what's planned for the rest of the day," Estella says.

I let out a sigh, lean against the wall, and close my eyes. Maybe I can rest a little before anything happens.

"You rest and if they come, I'll deal with them," she whispers, running her hand through my hair.

"You can't always be here to save me," I reply.

Estella has taken responsibility to help me anytime she can. She sees how much weight I've lost since being here and is worried about me. She has taken several beatings for me.

She can't save me from everything, but she has helped me dodge some beatings that saved my life. I don't know what I did to the guards and Mr. Rossi, but ever since he raped me the first time it's been horrible.

Mr. Rossi likes to have his way with me. Gives me to his guards and then has fun with me after. I tried fighting the first several times, but now I just lay there as they have their way with me. There isn't much I can do when there are four muscular guys against a malnourished girl.

I wish I could do something, but I learned the hard way the

first time the four guards raped me. They broke an arm and my collarbone. They had a doctor look me over and he gave me a brace, but they still made me work in the kitchen. I never got pain medicine and had to bite my lip or cheeks several times to get through the day.

I learned from that day onwards that I shouldn't fight back. It just makes me end up in more pain than necessary.

"If they continue to rape and beat you at this rate, you won't make it another month. I am trying to help you survive because I know your family and friends are coming to save you," Estella says.

I chuckle. "Sure."

"Just get some rest."

Estella stays silent after that, and all I can think about is my family. Are they coming for me? Have they forgotten about me?

So many thoughts run through my head. I try to get my mind off of my family. It makes me long for what I don't have.

Footsteps come closer to our cell. They sound different than the normal guard shoes. I freeze and open my eyes when I realize who it is.

Mr. Rossi.

Estella and I stand up, putting our heads down and hands behind our back. My whole body aches, but I push through the pain as I get into position.

Out of my peripherals, I see Mr. Rossi standing at the gate. He slowly unlocks the door and steps into our cell. I take in shallow breaths, trying to not move and get his attention. Maybe if I don't move, he won't pick me.

Sadly, that doesn't work as Mr. Rossi looks directly at me, and I curl in on myself. He can't want me again. He just had me several hours ago, and I am still healing. The last time he assaulted me and had a couple of other guys come in as well.

The other guys beat me some though, and my body hasn't healed yet.

"Take me," Estella steps in front of me.

I want to tell her no and that I'll go instead, but I know if I beg it will only be worse for one of us. Estella wasn't supposed to talk out of order. I know she'll get a good beating for that and I don't want to add onto it.

A wicked smile appears on Mr. Rossi's face.

"I'll get you next time." He looks directly at me.

Estella lets out a sigh of relief and follows Mr. Rossi out of the cell, leaving me alone to my thoughts. I drift back to when Mr. Rossi last had me earlier today.

"I'll never get tired of your body," he whispers in my ear.

I stay still, not wanting to anger him anymore than I already have.

I whimper in protest. Please, not my body again. It feels like you just used it a couple of minutes ago. I have a perpetual ache between my thighs and on my thighs.

"Hmm, maybe I'll have some fun another way." He walks around me. "The last guy I tortured only lasted an hour before his heart gave out."

My eyes go wide. Torture? I don't think I can do this. My body twitches, ready to run, but I have to tell myself that everything will be okay. He won't torture me. He only likes to rape me and be done.

"I think you can last longer than he did," Mr. Rossi whispers in my ear.

Sweat starts to form on my face as I take in his words. My body twitches again, but before I can react, Mr. Rossi has his hand around my neck.

"You don't get to run away from me. What I say will happen, and you are going to fucking obey," he growls.

I take in a shaky breath. Maybe he will get bored after an hour, if I last. I hope I don't last that long, I hope I die after a couple of minutes.

"I think I might enjoy whipping and cutting you." He pushes me to the ground. "After that, we'll see if you're still alive."

Before I can react, he has restraints on my wrists. I move my body, trying to get my feet free so I can kick him. Catching my foot, he clamps on a metal cuff before doing the other leg.

The chains are short and keep me in still. Tears brim my eyes when I realize I'm not getting out of this.

"Ah, look at the fire in your eyes dim." He chuckles. "My fucking favorite thing."

Mr. Rossi walks over towards the table and picks up a leather whip with tiny pins on the end. Fear courses through my veins as I watch him walk over towards me.

"Let's see how many I get to before you pass out," he says, walking behind me.

Without warning, the whip connects with my back. Pain radiates across my back as I feel each individual pin cut through my skin. I scream in pain, tears streaming down my face.

"Such a weak little human. I thought you wouldn't have screamed the first time," he whispers in my ear.

I take in a shaky breath. I don't know how many I can take before I pass out. I don't know how I am going to last through these and then the cuts from the knife.

My breathing picks up as I think through the events that happened. Black spots form in my vision and I try to blink them away. My breathing becomes shallow, my lungs begging me to let air in. With the torture playing through my mind, I pass out.

CHAPTER TEN

NOAH

Two months have passed since Marcy has been taken. It's been a hectic two months. Jillian is getting closer and closer to her due date.

Everyone has been on high alert. We have several people who are looking into it at all times of the day. A lot of people had to go back to work, or they would never get caught up.

It's been hard since Marcy has been taken. I don't know what to do with myself. I have tried helping find her, but I am not good with technology, and you can only scare so many people and get out all the information.

A lot of people saw the guys who took Marcy, but they were all wearing masks, so no one knows anything. Even if they were out in public, I don't think many people would have given them much thought. They are newcomers and us folk don't really pay attention to the newer people.

Since Marcy got taken, I've switched to being home-schooled so I can help around the club more. My dad didn't want me to, but once he realized that I wasn't going back to school he helped me switch.

I've been helping Jillian around the garage. Making sure she doesn't hurt herself carrying things. I didn't want to do this, but my dad said if I didn't want to go to school that I had to watch over Jillian. I want to go find who took Marcy, but my dad doesn't want me to get in trouble with the law.

She hasn't been the same since Marcy got taken away, and I completely understand that. No one is allowed to say anything about any leads in front of her. We don't want to get her hopes up again.

The first time Gears came home after asking around shops if they had seen anyone new and suspicious. He thought he had a lead until they looked into the guy, and it fell through.

Jillian didn't leave the garage much that time. She busied herself with work, tears in her eyes. She kept her mind busy with the cars and bikes.

Now, everything has to go through my dad or Bear before it can be said to Jillian. The doctor said that too much stress on her body can affect the baby and we don't want that.

"Can you pass me the wrench?" Jillian asks, breaking me from my thoughts.

Quickly picking up the wrench, I pass it to Jillian and watch her loosen a bolt. I look at Jillian's small frame. Apparently, she is bigger than she was with Marcy and some people are concerned.

Jillian has confided in me and told me that she doesn't want to live sometimes. I worry about her, but she says she is working through it, and it isn't all the time. I had told her that if I noticed anything serious, I would tell Bear or my dad.

I've made sure Jillian is eating when Bear isn't here to watch her. Bear didn't ask me to do that, but I know Marcy would want me to help out in any way that I can. We are also family, and we help family in times of need.

"Stop thinking and help me pick up this tire, Noah," Jillian grumbles.

I crack a smile and bend down. Picking up the tire, I watch Jillian point towards the corner of the garage. Placing the tire on the ground, I roll it over towards the corner of the room where all the other used tires are.

"Get a new tire," she yells.

I walk over and get one of the new tires. Jillian can be so bossy in the garage. I thought she was bossy before, but she is picky and super bossy while working. I wanted to quit the first day working with her because it was bad.

Gears had to tell me several times to take a deep breath and let it go. It's all the emotions going on right now. She isn't the same and I need to remember that. Fuck. None of us are the same. Everyone is on high alert.

I go to the gym every night and punch the shit out of the punching bags. Bear has let me start to use his little private gym because some of the guys are worried that I'll lash out and hurt them. After I go to the gym, I normally try to help Phantom out in any way, but that isn't much. I don't know technology like he does.

"Hurry up, Noah. I don't have all day," Jillian raises her voice.

"Technically, you do. This car isn't due for another three days," I reply.

I roll the tire back to Jillian and help put it on the car. Jillian has been so focused on work that they are actually ahead. Soon, she is going to run out of things to work on in here and it isn't going to be good. She won't know what to do and will be left to her thoughts.

"Shut up, fucker. I don't want to hear it," she grumbles.

I wince. Jillian has been cursing a lot more since Marcy got taken. It's like she is a whole different person. She used to be worried that the baby could hear her or anyone else curse and would manage everyone, but now it's like she doesn't care.

"Language." Gears walks into the room.

I give a little shake of my head towards Gears. He is going to start a fight. A fight I don't want to be here for. Bear tried telling her to watch her language and it was so bad. Bear eventually took Jillian to their house, and we didn't see them for a day.

Jillian stops what she's doing and glares at Gears, but that doesn't seem to faze him. We do this almost every day. He was used to her glares before she got pregnant, and Marcy got taken.

"I'll watch my fucking language when I want to," she snaps at him.

"Do I need to go have a convo with Bear again about your language? Think about the baby," he says.

"You don't need to talk to him. I'll watch my language."

Gears gives her a look of concern and watches her as she works. She normally fights harder than this, but maybe something happened between Bear and Jillian. They have been fighting more often.

"Noah, where are we on the schedule?" Gears asks, sitting down at his station.

"We are three days ahead of schedule," I reply.

If Jillian wasn't pregnant, I bet we would be further ahead, but I've been taking my time whenever she asks me to get things.

"I thought we were just a day ahead." Gears looks up at me, stunned.

I let out a little chuckle. "We were, but two of the days were pretty light and Jillian got them done."

He shakes his head and lets out a sigh. I would suggest calling all the people we told we didn't have space for and getting them booked, but I know that would be bad for Jillian. She is going to work herself to death if she continues to do this.

I take a step towards Gears.

"Do we need to get Bear?" I whisper, keeping an eye on Jillian.

"Maybe. Has she been like this all day?" he asks.

I nod my head and watch as Jillian tightens some nuts. She has taken a couple of breaks to eat food when I told her to. She has also gone to the bathroom several times.

"Let her finish this car, then we'll get Bear involved," he whispers. "Though, I don't think he'll be able to do much."

I don't know how much he will be able to do. He has asked her several times to not work as much, but she doesn't pay attention. I can understand why she works so much, but at the same time she is pregnant and if Marcy was pregnant with my child, I wouldn't want her to work.

"Ready for food?" Bear asks, walking into the garage.

Gears and I tense up, not expecting him to walk through the door. I look down at my watch and realize it has been several hours since Jillian and I last ate. Definitely time for her to eat again.

"Hey!" Gears says. "Jillian is almost done with the car."

Bear lets out a sigh and nods his head.

Jillian lets out a little squeak of pain, catching all three of us off guard. I turn around fast and watch as Jillian holds her back. I take a step forward, ready to help her, but Jillian glares at me.

"I don't need to be babied," she snaps.

"Jillian," Bear raises his voice.

"What!" she yells, facing him.

"Come here," he demands.

Jillian turns around and starts to work on the car again, completely ignoring everything Bear just said. I take a deep breath in, ready for them to start fighting. It seems like that's all they do right now, fight.

"Jillian," a warning comes from Bear.

She ignores him. I hear Bear take a deep breath in and wait for Jillian to stop.

"I understand that you want to work! Keep your mind off of things but you are fucking pregnant! You need to rest and think of the baby," Bear raises his voice. "You are going to hurt yourself. I'll never forgive myself if you get hurt when I could prevent it."

Jillian turns around, glaring at Bear. "You understand? I don't think you fucking do!"

"How do I not understand? Marcy is my daughter too!" he yells. "We are doing everything we can to get her back. I promise you."

"Talk to me when you find her or have news."

Everyone stops moving, but Jillian continues to work on the car. I have no clue what she is doing. Does she even realize what she just said?

"Baby, come on. Let's give your body a break from working. We don't want you to get hurt," Bear softly speaks to her.

"I know what I can and can't do. I've been pregnant before. This is no different from the time before," Jillian replies.

"Let's go relax in the clubhouse."

Jillian grabs onto my arm and bends down. "No."

"No?" Bear takes a step forward.

I wish I wasn't here right now. I would be so much happier if I didn't have to witness them fighting. I'm normally good about sneaking off when they start fighting, but Jillian still has a firm grip on my arm.

"I think it will be good if we relax. We both need some time together," Bear says.

"I can't," she replies.

"Can't or won't?"

She looks away from Bear, tightening her hold on me.

"Can't," her voice cracks.

Fuck me. She is about to cry. I don't do well with women crying.

"I think you don't want to. You don't want to leave and not be busy. We can talk, so there won't be silence. We can watch something. We can go shopping if you want." Bear takes a step closer to her.

She sniffles. I hope Bear comes over here before she starts crying. If Marcy ever started crying, I would hold her close to me. I don't think I would let her go until she told me everything was positively okay with her.

I feel helpless being in this garage when I know Marcy is somewhere out there. Several people have told me since we are on thin ice with the cops that I need to be careful and let Phantom handle everything. I don't like it and if they don't find her soon, I will be going out on my own, and finding her.

Bear places his hand against her back. Jillian quickly turns around and launches herself at him. Gears and I look at each other. I can see the longing in his eyes to have what they have. Even though Bear and Jillian fight, you can tell that they love each other.

Gears has been talking to Antoinette, but it's been hard. They have the same thing, but Antoinette is still so reserved, and I know it kills Gears.

"It's okay, baby. I'm right here. Let it all out," Bear whispers to Jillian.

They hold each other for a couple more seconds before Bear places her back on the ground.

"How about we go get some ice cream," Bear suggests.

"Okay," Jillian whispers.

Bear grabs onto Jillian's hand and leads her towards the exit of the garage.

"We'll see you tomorrow." Jillian waves at Gears and me.

"Take the day off! Relax and hang out with Bear," Gears says.

She shakes her head, but before she can reply, someone interrupts them.

"Wait! Bear! Jillian!" someone yells.

Everyone stops what they are doing and turns towards the voice. Phantom runs into the garage, out of breath.

"What is it?" Bear asks.

He takes a deep breath in. "I think I found something!"

CHAPTER ELEVEN

MARCY

I'm woken up by footsteps walking towards the cell. Huddled in a corner, I watch as a guard opens the door, two guards hold someone up behind him.

I don't move and keep my eyes mostly closed. I don't want them to know I'm awake. The guards tend to leave us alone if we are asleep.

"Throw her in here and we can leave," the guard holding the gate open says.

I watch as the two guards' step into the cell and throw the girl onto the ground. I flinch when her head bounces on the ground. That can't be good. She'll probably have a concussion from that.

The guards leave the cell, and I wait for the other guard to lock it. Every day, new guards come. Once they leave, I move as fast as I can towards the girl. I want to believe it isn't Estella, but I know it is.

No one else shares a cell with me. They don't bring new girls here. I stop right next to Estella and take everything in.

She is bloody and bruised. Her face is black and blue with streaks of red. Her eyes are swollen shut; her lips busted open in several places. I look down at her body. Her clothes are torn in several places. Bruises and small cuts litter her body.

A knot gets stuck in my throat. I want to cry for what they did to Estella. Why did Estella have to take my place? She shouldn't have. She should have been here all healed and not hurt because of me.

I gently place my hand on Estella's face, rubbing my thumb across her cheek. Estella moans and leans into my touch. I place my hands on her arms and help her sit up, her back against the bars.

Estella hisses as her back connects with the bars. She no doubt has several lashes on her back. That's what we normally get for speaking out of turn or taking each other's place. It hasn't happened many times, but if it's bad enough, you remember so you don't do it again.

"Oh, Estella," I choke out.

Estella gives me a small smile. She grimaces and falls limp against the bars. Her chest rising slightly and then falling.

"What did they do to you?" I whisper in horror.

I take in more of her body and notice burn marks. Gasping, I look closer at the burns before looking at her.

"Cigarettes," she mumbles.

Tears brim my eyes as I stare into her swollen eyes. Guilt washes over me, weighing me down. I should have spoken up when she got taken. I should have let them take me instead.

"You shouldn't have taken my place," I say, running my hands through her hair.

Estella opens her eyes and gives me a small smile. "I would do it again if given the opportunity."

I let out a tiny sob as I sit right next to her. My head snaps towards the right when footsteps sound in the building. With wide eyes, I frantically get up from my sitting position.

How am I going to get her to stand up? How is she going to

stand up in position, on her own? She can barely hold her head up.

I bend down, grabbing onto Estella's arms to help her up.

"I know it hurts. People are coming and I don't want you to get hurt anymore," I whisper

I try to pull her up, but I'm not strong enough. Tears brim my eyes as I try again. She doesn't deserve to get hurt again for not being able to stand up. It's not fair.

"Don't move the girl," someone says. "She won't get punished."

I snap my head towards the right and see the man that injected the birth control into me. My whole body is tense. I hope he doesn't pull a sick joke and punish her. You can never trust the people who work here.

The guard opens the door, letting the man into the room.

"I'm Dr. Smith, I am here to check Miss Estella over," he says, setting his bag onto the ground.

He takes a second to take in all of Estella before kneeling on the ground.

"You can sit beside her," he softly says.

I stare at him for a second, waiting for the guard to tell me no. Nothing is said, so I carefully sit next to Estella.

I watch the doctor look over Estella's face, touching it every once in a while.

"What a shame. Such a pretty face," the doc says.

The guard grunts before turning on his phone. It is such a shame. We shouldn't be here at all.

"Maybe someday you'll get out of here," he whispers.

Apparently not quiet enough because the guard's head snaps over towards us.

"What did you just say to them?" the guard raises his voice.

The doctor stops what he is doing and looks over at the guard.

"That someday they'll be out of here," he shrugs his shoulders.

Estella and I hold our breath. That's not something you say to the guards.

"They are our property. They stay with us until they die," the guard says. "If you know what's good for you, you'll stay quiet."

The doctor slightly nods his head and turns towards us. He gives us a small smile before he touches Estella's jaw. He opens it slightly and presses on a couple of places.

"Bruised. Not broken," he says.

The guard is now looking at the doctor, probably keeping a watchful eye on him. I wonder why the doctor said that in the first place.

"I'm lifting up your shirt to see your ribs," he says.

I watch him as he gently lifts her shirt and starts pressing down on them. Estella hisses when he presses down on her upper right side.

"They may be fractured. Take it easy for a couple of days and they should be fine." He moves to her left side and presses down.

Estella doesn't have a couple of days to take it easy. We no doubt have work tomorrow and they will probably beat us at some point as well.

"Maybe I can take you in for observation and let you heal fully before coming back to this nasty place," the doctor mumbles

"If I see you say anything other than medical stuff to the girls, I will kill you right here," the guard yells.

The doctor goes quiet and continues to work on Estella. He places her shirt back down before moving on to her legs.

Our uniforms are tight shirts and short shorts. The guards

and Mr. Rossi like to look at their artwork on our skins. All the bruises, cuts, burns, and more. It's disgusting.

I've seen several men get off on looking at all our marks. Commenting saying that it's sexy that we bare their marks on our skin. My skin crawls every time they say stuff like that.

"It looks like you are okay. Just make sure to take it easy on your ribs. Don't overexert yourself and get plenty of rest," he says.

We watch as he puts the few medical things back into his bag. He looks back at us before shaking his head.

"Take care of each other," he whispers, giving us a smile. "Stay safe and I may come back for you two."

Before anyone could do anything, the guard pulls out his gun and shoots the doctor in the head. Estella and I scream as blood splatters all over us. I stand there in shock, not able to look away from the dead doctor.

"When I say not to do something, you fucking listen to me," the guard barks out.

I nod my head with understanding. Estella and I already knew that. We have learned the hard way to follow orders.

Two guards make their way into our cell, grabbing the doctor and dragging him out. Estella and I watch as they drag him away from us, leaving a trail of blood behind.

"We'll get you some stuff to clean up with," a guard mumbles.

They lock the door and make their way out of the building, coming back several minutes later with a bucket and rags.

"This better be cleaned before we come back," he says.

The guards leave and I get started on cleaning Estella and me first. Once I'm done cleaning us, I start working on the floors. I may get in trouble for cleaning us, but it's a risk I am willing to take. Blood is sticky and it will only get worse the longer we let it stay on us.

"I'm gonna clean you now," I whisper.

I pull the bucket of water closer to Estella and dunk the rag in it. Wringing it out, I gently clean away the blood on her face and arms. Once I am done with her, I start to clean myself. I finish rather quickly, not wanting to prolong cleaning the floor.

I don't know when they are coming back, and I want it done as soon as possible. It would be easier if Estella was helping me, but she is too hurt, it would only make things worse.

Splashing some water on the ground, I start to scrub, losing myself in my thoughts.

* * *

Hours have passed since the doctor came into the cell. The guards just came to give us bread and water while taking the bucket and rags away. Estella doesn't want to eat, and it's my turn to step up and feed her.

I've been helping her out since the doctor came. She had to go to the bathroom, so I helped her get to the bucket. I didn't want her to be humiliated like I was when I had to pee myself. It took us several minutes to get her up. A lot of crying and pain, but we made it happen.

"Just a little bit. You need something in your stomach," I whisper, breaking off a piece of bread.

I hold the bread up to her mouth and wait for her to take it. Her jaw is severely bruised, but not broken. She takes the little piece of bread and slowly chews.

"That's it. Just a couple more and then you can rest," I say.

I take a couple of small bites before giving her another piece of bread. We do this for a while before the bread and water is gone. It looks like tonight is going to be a quiet night and I can't wait. Maybe both of us can get some much-needed sleep before tomorrow.

"Let's get you comfortable so you can sleep," I whisper.

Standing up, I help Estella get into a comfortable position on the ground. I'm hoping she can at least get some sleep. She desperately needs it after today's beating.

I sit back down and lean my back against the wall. Closing my eyes, I feel myself drifting off to sleep.

Hands wrap around my arms, yanking me forward. I let out a scream as their fingernails dig into my arm. Looking up at the person, I see a guard I've never seen before.

"Marcy!" Estella screams.

I turn my head as I get dragged out of the cell. Estella is trying to get up but isn't strong enough.

"Marcy!" she cries out.

Something overcomes me, and I try to fight against the person. I don't know what possessed me to do it.

"Shut up, bitch," he sneers.

I shake my arm, trying to get out of his hold. His grip tightens on my arm, making me whimper in pain.

The guy drags me up the stairs and into the dark night. I can't make anything out. My breathing quickens when I realize I can't win a fight against this guy.

"Please," I beg.

The guy grunts and continues to drag me into the house. Guards stare at us with wicked smiles when they see me getting dragged. Some even cheer when they see me struggle against his grip. Bile rises up my throat. All of them are sick.

We make our way up the stairs and walk down a long hallway. The guy stops in front of the furthest door and opens it. Pushing me into the room, I stumble and fall to the ground.

I look up at him as he stalks towards me, my eyes wide with panic.

CHAPTER TWELVE

JILLIAN

I stare at Phantom in shock. After two months, he finally has something on my daughter? I rip myself out of Bear's hold and quickly move towards Phantom.

"Careful, baby mama. We don't want you to trip over something and get hurt." Bear wraps his arms around me.

I let out a sigh and nod my head. It would be bad for me to get hurt and not hear what Phantom has to say. I carefully walk the rest of the way, stopping right in front of Phantom.

"Well?" I ask, looking up at him.

"Follow me," he replies.

Bear, Gears, Noah, Butch, and I follow Phantom as we walk towards his office. I hope and pray that it's all good news and we will have our daughter back in our arms soon. I've missed her so much.

Bear holds the door open as everyone walks into Phantom's office. I've only been in here a handful of times, and it still shocks me how big this place is.

He has several monitors up and running. Some showing videos from security cameras and some where he does all his work. It's all neat, like someone hasn't touched anything in over a year after cleaning it.

"Okay, you can sit here," Phantom says, pulling out a chair for me.

I let out a sigh but give Phantom a smile. I hate getting special treatment, but at the same time I am grateful. My feet have been killing me and all I've wanted to do for the past several hours is sit and relax.

I sit down and can't help but let out a little moan when all the pressure is off my feet. This feels absolutely amazing.

Everyone chuckles but Bear. He's staring at me with hunger in his eyes, but there is a sliver of worry in them.

"Are you okay?" he asks, placing a hand on my shoulder.

"Yeah. Just feels good to be off my feet," I say and give him a smile.

He glares at me and sighs. "We'll talk later."

I give him a smile before turning to Phantom. Bear has been getting onto me for being on my feet too much. Sometimes I agree with him, but it's been hard to sit and do nothing. My thoughts get to me, and I can get some too scary thoughts since Marcy has been taken.

"Alright before we go to my screen, it took me a while to track the cars they used. They used three different cars to move her. It also took me a while to figure out who the cars were under. All different aliases, but the person wasn't that good at hiding their real identity." Phantom sits down in his chair.

We all stare at him, ready for him to say more.

"Who was the guy?" Noah asks impatiently.

"I'm getting to that. It's some Italian dude that should be dead. Anyway, they crossed state lines. That was harder to track, but I managed to get into the cameras in that state. They thought they were being good about not getting in front of cameras, but every time they changed cars, it was caught on camera," Phantom says, turning on his computer.

I start to feel anxious the longer he talks. I just want to know if Marcy is okay. I just want to hear the words *she is alright*.

I watch as Phantom starts to pull several things up on his computer. I stare at the screen, trying to catch any glimpse of if Marcy is okay or not.

"They took her to this abandoned facility, and I haven't seen them leave. I looked into it and apparently there are underground tunnels that lead all over," Phantom says. "So, I decided to look into Jared. I just had this weird feeling about him."

I give Phantom a confused look. Jared has been dead for years. What could he possibly have to do with this? He couldn't have known that I was going to be pregnant or where Marcy would be.

"He's dead," I whisper.

"Yes, he is, but how did he get out of prison?" Phantom asks.

How did Jared get out of prison? I've always asked myself that question but never found out. I don't think I really wanted to know how he got out. I was satisfied knowing he was dead and couldn't come after me anymore.

"Who got him out of prison?" Gears asks.

"The Italian Mafia," Phantom says, pulling up a screen with mugshots.

I stare at all of them, but none of them look familiar.

"The Italian Mafia? How did Jared get mixed up with the Italian Mafia?" I ask, looking at Phantom.

"Did Jared ever sell drugs? Was he gone for a couple days at a time and would come home with money?" Phantom asks me.

I think back to when I lived with him. I don't ever remember him selling drugs, but he did leave a lot. He always had money and never worried about running out.

"No, to the drugs, but yes to him leaving and coming back with money," I say.

"He worked with the Italian Mafia for years. A couple of years before he met you, up until he died," Phantom informs me.

"The Italian Mafia has Marcy?" I choke out, tears appearing in my eyes.

Are we ever going to get Marcy back from them? I've heard crazy things about the Mafia, and I don't want anything to do with them, but I want my daughter back.

"Yes, they do have her," Phantom says.

I let out a sob, my body shaking from everything.

"H-how are we going to get her back? Can we get her back?" I shakily ask.

"I have a source that is in the Italian Mafia. We made contact with him and he is going to call us later to give us details," Phantom says.

Everyone stares at him in shock. A source in the Italian Mafia? How did we manage to do that? Relief floods through me when I hear him say that. Am I going to be able to get my daughter back?

"How do we know we can trust this source? This is my daughter's life on the line," Bear says.

"Yeah! For all we know, they could be double crossing us. People want us dead," Noah raises his voice.

"This does not leave the room. Understood?" Phantom looks at everyone.

"Yes," we all say together.

"Our source is Dom. Only Pres and I knew he went undercover."

Dom? Who the hell is Dom? Then it clicks.

"Wait, Dom as in our Dom?" I ask, barely a whisper. "The one who left fifteen years ago?"

Phantom gives me a small smile. "The one and only."

"I thought he was in Arizona helping out our brother MC," Gears says.

"He was and still technically is. We thought it was best that he went straight into the Italian Mafia to be a spy," Phantom replies. "We didn't want to risk him being seen at the other MC's compound before he went undercover."

"How has he done this for fifteen years?" I whisper to myself.

"The first couple of years were super hard, it still is, but he is used to it more now. He's had to do some pretty messed up things, but he knows it's for a better cause."

He's missed all these years of finding someone for him. The special person he will love and cherish for the rest of his life.

Tears appear in my eyes the longer I think about this. He's missed out on so much. Seeing Marcy grow up and being around his MC brothers.

"It's going to be okay. He volunteered for this. He knew what he was signing up for," Phantom says.

"He knew he was the most qualified to do this," Gears mumbles.

I shake my head, trying not to think about this. If I continue to think about this, I'm just going to turn into a blubbering mess.

"So, what do you have so far?" Bear asks.

"Right. The intel we have so far. This guy Lorenzo Rossi is the head of the Mafia. Luca is his right hand," Phantom says, pointing to each person's mug shot.

"Where does Dom fit into this?" Butch asks, finally speaking up.

"He has made his way up the chain, the past fifteen years. He's had to do some pretty fucked up things, but it's paid off. We have a lot to blackmail the Italian Mafia with, though I'm hoping it never comes to that," Phantom says. "He's currently the fourth in command."

"So, well trusted," Gears points out.

"Yes, very well trusted."

I stay quiet, trying to process everything that has just been said. We've been lied to this whole time where Dom was so he could be a spy for us in the Italian Mafia. He can help get our daughter back.

"When will we know more?" I ask.

"It could be at any point. Dom calls when he knows it's safe to call," Phantom replies.

I don't know how long I can wait with this information. I just want to know now when we will get our baby back. It's going to kill me knowing we can have her back at any second or in several months.

"I know it's hard, but we have to keep this quiet. No one can know that he is there," Phantom says.

I nod my head really fast. Excitement bubbles in me. I'm getting my daughter back. She'll be with us once again.

"I'll keep you updated if I find anything else out," Phantom says, turning towards us.

"Thanks," Butch and Gears say, walking out of the room.

Noah stays silent and continues to look at the screen. I watch him as he looks over Lorenzo and Luca's face, almost like he is committing them to memory. I'll have Bear talk to him later about that. I don't want him to do anything irrational, or mess things up.

I know Noah cares about Marcy a lot, probably loves her. I don't want him to do something that he will regret for the rest of his life or get himself killed. I know it would devastate Marcy if she found out he died trying to save her.

"Sounds good. Thank you," Bear says, bringing me out of my thoughts.

"Thanks," I whisper.

Bear helps me stand up. I wince when all the weight is on my feet again. Looking down, I realize that my ankles are swollen.

"Let's go relax," I say, wrapping my arms around his waist.

Bear and I walk out of Phantom's office and towards our room. I wince every once in a while, when I put too much force into my steps.

Without warning, I am up in the air. I let out a little scream in shock.

"Bear!" I scold him. "Give me a warning next time."

"Next time, tell me you are hurting and maybe I won't pick you up without warning," he fires back at me.

"It's not a long walk. I could have made it."

"Get this through your thick skull. Next time you will fucking tell me that your feet are hurting and swollen. I will carry you."

"I'm not a child," I mumble.

"You are when you don't pay attention to me. I want you healthy. I want this baby healthy. If you keep walking on your feet too much and making them swollen, you are going to hurt yourself."

I let out a sigh. He does have a point, but I'm not going to let him have the satisfaction of knowing that.

Bear enters our room and lays me down on the bed. I let out a sigh of content as I snuggle into the bed. So fucking comfortable. Bear gently takes off my shoes and pulls the covers over me.

He walks around the bed and gets in behind me, wrapping his arms around me.

"You're going to be the death of me," he mumbles.

I let out a little chuckle and snuggle into his arms. I relax and take everything in.

"We're getting our baby back," I whisper.

"Baby, I'm excited, but don't get your hopes up that it will be the next day we get her back. It could take a couple of weeks or more," Bear replies, rubbing his hand against my pregnant belly.

"I know. I just can't believe we are getting her back."

Bear kisses my shoulder and pulls me tighter to him. Closing my eyes, I fall asleep in Bear's arms.

CHAPTER THIRTEEN

MARCY

"Get up, bitch," he barks out.

Fear courses through my veins as I scramble to get up and move into position. I feel his hands wrap around my neck, squeezing slightly, making it harder to breathe. I open my mouth and try to take a breath of air, but it's so hard.

"Please, don't," I whisper.

He chuckles and pushes me backwards, my back landing on the bed. I scramble backwards as he stalks towards me. Panic courses through me the closer he gets.

"Please, I'll do anything. Just don't rape me," I beg.

I try to get up from the bed to get onto my knees. Maybe if I kneel in front of him, he will have mercy on me. I don't think I can go through with this again. My back is still hurting from the whips and cuts.

He stops in his tracks and stares at me. I push that to the back of my mind. Maybe he is waiting to see what I will do before he decides. Hear everything I have to say before picking one. One other guy did that to me, and I ended up having to do everything I blurted out to him, but it got me out of being raped. Just for a couple hours until the next guy came in.

"I'll give you a blow job. I'll let you whip me. I'll let you do anything else but rape me. Please," I plead.

I quickly move off of the bed when he doesn't move from his spot. I scramble closer to his body.

"I'll give you a bath, and a blow job," I fall onto my knees, the pain in the back of my mind.

With shaky hands, I bring them up towards his pants to unbuckle them. A hand lands on my shoulder, making me scream in pain and shock. The touch is gentle, something I haven't felt in a long time.

My whole body shakes as I wait for him to hit me. My brain works overtime thinking about all the things I did wrong. I spoke out of turn. I begged him to do something else. I got out of position. I started something that he never said he wanted.

A sob makes its way through my mouth the longer he waits to say something. What is he going to do to me?

"Look up," he whispers.

I slowly look up, making eye contact with him. He gives me a small smile before cupping my cheek with his hand. I freeze, the feeling so foreign to me.

No man since I got here has been gentle with me.

"Please," I whisper.

He shakes his head and takes a step back. I cry as he walks away. He is going to get stuff to hurt me with. I can feel it in my bones.

"Sit on the bed," he says.

I slowly get up from the ground and make my way over to the bed, sitting at the edge. I keep my eyes on him, waiting for him to strike back at any second.

"I'm sorry. Please don't punish me," I plead.

He doesn't pay any attention to me. Tears continue to stream down my face. I blink several times, trying to get the tears out of my eyes so I can keep watching him.

The mysterious guy walks across the room, grabbing a chair and bringing it over towards me.

"I can give you a lap dance," I blurt out.

I've never given one, but maybe he will agree to this and not rape me. I could definitely give a lap dance over him using my body.

He picks up a notebook and pen before sitting down. I clamp my mouth shut. What is he doing? Is he going to stab me with that pen? Cut me with the pieces of paper?

A shiver makes its way through my body at those thoughts. That would hurt so much. Phantom pain runs down my arms, making me rub my arms.

The man starts to write in the book before scooting closer to me. I watch him warily, wondering what he is doing. He moves the book towards me, and I flinch.

I look up at the guy, but his eyes are on the paper. I look back down, as he moves the notebook closer to me. Taking it in my shaky hands, I look down at the words written.

I'm not here to hurt you. Be quiet and I'll explain everything.

I stare at the words, not fully taking them in. I reread the two sentences several times before my brain catches up. He isn't here to hurt me? Then what is he doing here? There are no nice guys here. They are all vile and dangerous.

I look back up at the guy, taking in his appearance. He looks well kept, not like the other guards. Who is this guy?

"W-who are you?" I whisper.

He gives me a small smile. "I'm Dom, and I know your parents."

My mouth hangs open. What? He knows my parents. Why

is he here? Is he turning against my parents? Is he going to take them down and hurt me later?

"It's okay. Calm down for me. I'm not going to hurt you or them," he whispers.

He stays in his seat, looking at me.

"How do I know you really know my parents? I've never seen you in my life or pictures of you," I say.

He chuckles and shakes his head. "You are just like your mother. I've got a picture of all of us when you were a baby."

He pulls his phone out of his pocket and starts swiping. He turns his phone around, showing a picture. I take a close look and realize that it's my parents, Dom, and me. I'm wrapped up in a blanket, my baby blanket.

"Why are you here?" I ask skeptically.

"I left when you were two years old. Oh man, you loved me. Anytime I walked in the room, you would scream until I held you," he sighs. "The Italian mafia kept bothering our brother MC in Arizona, so they sent me to be a spy in the mafia."

"For fifteen years?!" I whisper yell.

He flinches and nods his head. "Yeah, for fifteen years. I've gotten a lot of dirt on them. Make contact with your dad once a month. I didn't know you were here until Phantom contacted me."

I give him a small smile. "That's a long time."

"Yeah, it is. I'm hoping once I get you out that I can go back to the MC. I've missed everyone."

"I bet. Sorry you had to do this for fifteen years."

"I would do it again if it meant I could help you here. Sorry I didn't know sooner."

"It's okay."

He shakes his head.

"It's really not. I heard there was a new girl here. Related to an MC but didn't know which one. I tried to figure out who it was, but they kept me busy the past two months. I didn't know until Phantom contacted me," he says.

"Not your fault," I murmur.

"I know what they did to you. They've been talking about it a lot," his voice breaks.

"You're here now. That's what matters."

"Sorry for also being rough on you. Had to keep up an image so I wouldn't get caught."

"It's okay."

I completely understand why he did everything now. People were probably listening in to hear me. It's happened several times. Some guards have a game to see who can make me scream the loudest.

Dom couldn't let me in on anything in case I slipped up. I wonder if I will be able to keep it up after we leave this room. I clear my thoughts of that. Of course, I am going to keep it up that he did stuff to me. We can't risk anything.

We sit in silence for a little bit. I look around the room, taking everything in. It's actually a nice room. It's very spacious and has a dresser and a bathroom. Everything is either black or grey, but it goes so well together.

The bed is comfortable. I don't think my bed at home is even this comfortable. It's like sitting on a bed of clouds or feathers. You just sink into it and get comfortable.

I could sleep here for several days and not get tired of it. I wish Estella and I could sleep on this. I think Estella has forgotten what a bed feels like. She has been here since she was very little and has always slept on the concrete floor.

Dom chuckles, taking me out of my thoughts. I look at him and tilt my head. Why is he laughing?

"That boyfriend of yours is a real spitfire," he says.

"Why do you say that?" I ask.

"I was on the phone with him and Phantom. He is furious

that you got taken. Threatened me that if I fucked this up, he would come after me, brother or not."

I stare at Dom in shock. Did Noah really say that? That is so unlike him to say stuff like that.

"Never heard him talk like that before?" Dom asks.

I shake my head, still in shock.

"You've got yourself a keeper. He will do absolutely anything for you. You tell him to kill a person and he will. Jump off a cliff and he will ask when and where," he chuckles.

"Not funny," I grimace.

I don't like talking about him dying. Never have and never will like it.

"I'm serious. He will fucking kill anyone for you. You mean the world to him, and I don't even know him that well." Dom shakes his head.

I just stare at Dom, not knowing what to say. What do you say to that? I'm happy that Noah will do anything to get me back, but at the same time I'm shocked. I get butterflies in my stomach saying he would kill anyone for me, but at the same time I don't want him to.

"I know that look on your face. You're happy that he would kill anyone for you," Dom says.

"I guess. Does that make me a bad person?" I ask.

Dom laughs. "No."

I let out a little breath, not completely satisfied with that. I'll have to continue to think about that. See if I actually am happy Noah would kill someone for me. He has never shown that side of himself to me before, so it's all new.

"Okay, I'm working on getting you out. I am talking with your dad and Phantom soon, to come up with a plan," he says.

Tears brim my eyes. I can't believe that I may get out of here soon. I'll be free again.

"What about Estella?" I stare at him with wide eyes. "I'm not leaving without her."

Estella hasn't been outside of this compound since she was very little. It's not fair for me to get taken out and be free, and she can't.

"Who is Estella?" he asks.

"The other girl that was in my cell with me," I say.

"Yes, it will make it more difficult, but we will make it work that both of you get out."

I let out a sigh of relief. I can't wait to tell her about this. It's going to be amazing.

"I know that face. You can't tell the other girl," he says.

"Why? She deserves to know," I reply.

"The fewer people who know, the better. I promise that I will get both of you out. I just need it to stay between us."

"Okay."

He lets out a breath of air. He stands up from the chair.

"I promise I will get both of you out," he says.

I quickly jump up from my sitting position and fling myself at him, hugging him.

"Thank you," I whisper.

CHAPTER FOURTEEN

MARCY

Dom and I freeze our movements when we realize I'm hugging him. I don't know what came over me to hug him. I've been so good these past two months of doing what I'm told and not being out of line.

I start to pull away, but his arms wrap around me, hugging me back. I feel his hand slip into my back pocket, but I don't think anything of it.

"Sorry," I whisper.

"Nothing to be sorry for. Just caught me off guard," he replies, letting me go.

I pull away from him. What did I just do? I know he is part of the MC, but this is so out of character for me.

"I shouldn't have done that. I'm sorry. I wasn't given permission to hug you." I step away from him.

Panic courses through my veins. My breathing picks up and all the noise disappears. With wide eyes, I look up at Dom and back away. I shouldn't have done that. The punishment I'll get when people find out.

I don't know if I can withstand another punishment like

that. Last time, it almost killed me, and they were being generous with the punishment. They said the next time I got one of those punishments that it would be worse.

My back hits the wall behind me. I slide down and bring my legs up to my chest. I gasp for breath, not able to get any air in. My chest tightens with panic, black dots appearing in my vision.

I see a blurry figure walking towards me. I press myself more into the wall, trying to get away.

"Please," I rasp out.

My hand goes to my neck, clawing at it. I just want to take a breath in. I want this panic to go away.

The figure continues to walk closer to me, and I frantically look around the room, trying to find an exit but not being able to see one through the blur.

Pain erupts on my neck, but I pay no attention to it and continue to claw at it. I start to feel lightheaded and dizzy.

Hands appear on my shoulders, and I thrash, trying to get out of them.

"No," I gasp.

The hands stay on my shoulders and start to move me. I scramble, trying to get away, but the hands are too strong. My head connects with something solid, and I can start to feel a heartbeat.

Hands run through my hair, and I can feel vibrations through the body. My mind starts to calm down and my body lets me take in small little breaths.

"It's okay," the person mumbles.

Their voice sounds so far away, but I know they are right next to me. They sound like they are underwater. They continue to run their hands through my hair, keeping my head firmly placed against the chest. A chest? Why is my head on a person's chest?

I feel the panic start to come again. I shouldn't be on

anyone's chest besides Estella's. She sometimes lets me fall asleep with my head on her chest, but this is a male's chest.

"Please, no," I whisper.

I try to get away, but the arms hold me tight against them.

"Please, no! Let me go!" I yell.

I want to be free. I shouldn't have my head on their chest. They shouldn't be running their hands through my hair. They shouldn't be so nice to me. I don't deserve it. I haven't done anything to deserve this.

"It's okay. Just calm down," the voice says.

The person starts to rock back and forth while they continue to hold me tight against them. My body starts to relax as the person continues to rock. My breathing starts to become normal, my hearing and vision slowly come back.

"It's going to be okay. I'm not going to hurt you," Dom mumbles.

His hands continue to run through my hair and down my back. I come back to all of my senses and completely relax against Dom.

"How are you feeling?" he asks.

I shrug my shoulders, not wanting to speak. My neck fucking hurts from all the scratching I did. I wouldn't be surprised if I drew some blood. I just want to relax a little more before I have to go back to my reality.

"I can't say I know what you went through, cause I've never had one of them, but you aren't alone," he mumbles. "You've been through hell here."

I continue to listen to his heartbeat, completely ignoring the words he says to me.

"Okay, we probably need to head back now. We've been here a while and some of the guys will get suspicious," he says, bringing me out of my little bubble.

I gently pull myself away from him and stand up. I watch as

he stands to his full height and rolls his shoulders back. He is so much taller than me, and if he wasn't from the MC and wanted his way with me, he could totally force himself on me and I wouldn't stand a chance.

"It feels wrong to even say this, but we have to keep up the image that I had my way with you," he says, flinching towards the end. "I'm gonna need to slap you real hard on the face to show that I did something to you."

I nod my head slowly. I knew this would happen. He says he's sorry, and it feels wrong to say it, but does he really mean it? Don't most guys want their way with a girl? Be their personal punching bag?

"I'm gonna need you to also ruffle up your clothes to make it look like you got roughed up a little and your hair," he continues to talk.

I nod my head for the second time. I can do that. I kind of remember what my clothes look like after the men have their way with me. Ruffling up my clothes and hair, I look back up towards Dom.

"Okay, now I'm gonna slap you in the face real hard. I'm so sorry I have to do this. It pains me knowing that I have to live with this for the rest of my life," he says.

I hold my stance, bracing myself for the hit. I watch him as he raises his hand and I close my eyes. The palm of his hand comes crashing down onto my cheek. My lip cracks open, blood pooling and rolling down my chin.

My head flings towards the right with the force. Pain radiates across my cheek. I can feel his hand still on my cheek, throbbing, but I know it's not there. He just hit me that hard.

Opening my eyes, I look up at Dom. Sadness fills his face as he takes in what he did to me. I swear I could see his eyes get glossy, but he blinks, and his face goes void of any emotion.

"I'm gonna need to drag you out of here like I dragged you in here," he tells me.

I nod my head slowly, not really comprehending his words. It's like my emotions know when things are going to happen and just shut off. My body just shuts down when it starts getting hurt. Knowing that I shouldn't fight back.

He grabs onto my upper arm with a tight grip that makes me wince in pain. Without warning, he yanks on my arm, making me fall to the ground. My knees hit the ground really hard, making me bite my busted lip and break even more skin.

I hold in a groan of pain as he jerks my arm again to get up. It's like a switch in him flips, and he isn't a friendly person anymore. I know he has his image to uphold, but he doesn't have to be a complete asshole.

He opens the door and drags me out of the room. We make our way through the long hallway and towards the stairs.

We start our descent down the stairs; me tripping on almost every step. Dom grunts a couple of times and just yanks my arm. The closer we get to the bottom, the more voices I hear talking. I stiffen, afraid that they will want their way with me.

Dom pulls me into the big room where all the people are. He makes his way towards the exit everyone takes.

"Hey, Rio! You were up there a long time with that bitch!" one guard yells.

Dom stops his movements and stares at him.

"Couldn't get enough of her," he replies, cracking a smile.

Everyone laughs and stares at me hungrily. A shiver runs through my body in disgust, but all the men take it a different way. Their smiles widen and they continue to eye my whole body.

"I can't get enough of her. I think I fuck her at least four times a week," another guard chimes in.

"I try to have her at least once a day," the first guard says. "Good thing the bitch is on birth control. Wouldn't want her to get pregnant."

"Wouldn't be your first time to get someone pregnant. You'll just beat them until they have a miscarriage," a deep voice says.

I stare at the man with wide eyes. He beats the girls and makes them have miscarriages? That's awful and should never be allowed.

"Oh yeah, and I enjoy it every time. Watching the blood coat their legs and the horror in their eyes when they realize they've lost the baby," he chuckles.

I start to feel nauseous the longer the guy talks. He is the worst one of them all. He shows no mercy when he rapes us. Everyone is afraid of him. I've learned to just let him do anything and not fight back, especially with him. That's one way to get yourself killed.

Everyone chuckles and agrees that it's amazing to watch the blood run down their legs. Some guards start to chime in that they like to stick things up their pussy to block it and then hit them, keeping a lot of the blood up there.

Bile starts to rise in my throat, and I do everything I can to keep it down. Not the time to puke.

Dom starts to move towards the exit, and I mindlessly follow, not really paying attention. I'm trying everything in me to not puke.

"We didn't hear her screams. What'd you do to keep her so quiet?" one guard asks, bringing me out of my thoughts. "It's always fun to hear her scream, begging for us to stop."

"I gagged her. Her pleas were getting on my nerves," Dom replies with a chuckle.

"Good idea! I'll have to try that the next time I have my way with her."

"I'm never gagging her. I love to hear her beg me to stop.

Makes me so fucking hard that I continue to relentlessly fuck her. Best time of my fucking life," a different guard says.

Dom stiffens and laughs before he continues to drag me out of the house. I have a hard time keeping up with Dom. I trip several times, falling to the ground and hurting my knees.

"Sorry," he mumbles.

I know he can't show that he cares about me. That would give everything away and we wouldn't be able to escape. We all have to put up a mask and pretend like he raped and beat me.

We make our way into the other house, walking down the stairs and towards my cell. A guard unlocks the door and opens it for Dom.

Before I can even comprehend what is happening, I feel my body being thrown into the air. My body hits the concrete floor, pain radiating all over my body. I groan in pain.

Once the cell door is closed and locked, Estella comes over towards me. She helps me sit up and get comfortable against the wall.

"I'm okay," I whisper.

She sits right next to me, holding my hand. Her head leans onto my shoulder. I lay my head on hers, closing my eyes, but remember that Dom put his hand in my back pocket. Moving slightly, I push my hands into my back pocket and feel the paper.

I pull it out and uncrinkle the paper and read it.

"I'm coming for you, baby. I love you," I whisper.

I hope this note is from Noah. I don't know who else it would be from.

"What's that?" Estella whispers, curiosity laces her voice.

"A note. I think it's from Noah," I reply.

"It probably is. I don't want to know how you got it in case someone comes in and asks about it. Now, let's get some sleep."

I put the paper back into my pocket and get comfortable.

My mind is racing with thoughts, but I force myself to stop and fall asleep.

CHAPTER FIFTEEN

BEAR

I stare at Jillian as she sleeps in our bed. She looks so peaceful as she lies on her side, her pregnant belly on display. I could watch her sleep and never get bored.

I let out a sigh, getting up from my chair, and walking out of the room. The whole time Phantom was talking, I just had a feeling that he wasn't telling us everything. I don't know if it was because Jillian was there or if he just wasn't allowed to say anything.

Walking down the stairs, I watch everyone in the main room chatting and talking to each other. Maybe Jillian and I should go and talk with them after I'm done with Phantom. I think it would be good for Jillian to relax and talk with people.

She's been keeping to herself lately, working in the garage with Gears and Noah. She had to stop working as one of the bartenders, because I wanted more time with her. Whiskey was not happy when she told him that, but she promised she would help out every once in a while.

I didn't like her telling him that, but I have to pick and choose my battles. She was willing to stop working if she could help every once in a while. Now that she is pregnant, she hasn't helped much at all. Her feet get swollen super-fast and Whiskey has banned her.

I stop in front of his office door and knock.

"Come in," he says.

Opening the door, I look around the room and stop. Why is Noah still in here?

"He just came back," Phantom says.

"What are you doing here?" I ask Noah.

"I wanted more answers. I want to get Marcy back just as much as you do," Noah replies.

I stare into Noah's eyes, trying to see if he is telling the truth. He's a good kid, but is he good enough for my daughter?

"Do you love my daughter?" I ask.

His eyes go wide, and his mouth is open. Phantom starts to mumble something, but I ignore him and continue to stare at Noah.

His mouth opens and closes several times. Annoyance starts to bubble up. Maybe he isn't right for my daughter if he can't even answer me.

"Well?" I cross my arms.

"Y-," his voice cracks.

Phantom winces as Noah clears his throat.

"Yes, I do love your daughter. Have for a while," he says, staring right into my eyes.

"Good," I reply.

Noah stares at me in disbelief as I grab a chair and pull it up next to him.

"If you hurt my daughter, I will fucking torture you until you beg for death," my voice goes an octave lower.

Fear flashes through his eyes and his facial expression as his face goes white. People have heard about me torturing people and how I keep them on the brink of death for days. I never let those fuckers die easy. They deserve everything they get from me.

"Yes, sir," he replies.

Satisfied with his answer, I sit down in the chair. I relax in my chair and look over at Phantom. I take in his body language, trying to figure out if he truly is hiding something. He is on guard, stiff and not showing any emotion. What is he keeping from us?

"You withheld information," I say, placing my right ankle on my left knee.

I lean back into my chair, feeling victorious when I see Phantom's eyes go wide. He quickly regains his composure and sits up straight.

"I was not withholding information," he says. "I just couldn't say it in front of Jillian."

"Why?" I ask.

What information could he say that Jillian can't hear? Is something wrong with Marcy? Is it more complicated than he originally thought it was and he didn't want to say anything?

"I have a layout of the place and have gotten some surveillance, but nothing great to go off of," Phantom says. "I didn't want to add any more stress for Jillian."

Jillian has been stressed lately, and if she stresses anymore, the doctor said she could be put on bed rest. I know that would kill Jillian to be confined to her bed. She's always moving around and has to be doing something.

If she ever got put on bed rest, I would probably have to handcuff her to the bed to make sure she stayed there.

"What have you done with the layout of the place and surveillance video?" I ask.

"I haven't done much with it yet. Haven't had time. I got it an hour before I told you guys everything," he replies.

Of course he hasn't done much with it yet.

"I was marking it up where the guards stand, cameras are, and all the exits. I was going to show it to you eventually," Phantom says.

"When is eventually?" I ask, anger showing in my voice.

Why didn't he text me after I left? Why didn't he give me a signal that he wanted to talk to me? He should have said something to me and not waited hours after when I came to him.

"I was about to text you. I didn't want to disturb your time with Jillian. I thought she would find it suspicious that you got a text from me right after we met," he says.

He looks in a panic when he says all of that. I can understand why. No one wants to get on my angry side. I don't think as rationally as I do when I'm not angry. Jillian always scolds me when I start to get angry and yell at people.

I take a deep breath in like Jillian would tell me if she was here. I will get more accomplished if I keep my anger under control.

"Can I see the layout of the place?" I ask.

Phantom blinks at me, not moving. I stare at him, waiting for him to either pull it up or give me a piece of paper, but all he does is sit there.

"Well?" I ask impatiently.

"Sorry," he says.

I watch as he pulls open a drawer and rummages through things. For having a clean office, he sure does just pile things into his drawer. It's so messy in there, you probably can't find anything.

"Kind of messy," I mumble.

Phantom shoots me a glare. "I've been fucking busy trying to find your daughter. I can't keep everything clean."

I let out a little chuckle. Damn right he can't. I think this is the first time I've seen something so messy that came from him. He's always so clean and organized.

"It's been killing me knowing that it's messy, but I've pushed it away so I can find Marcy," he says.

"Thanks," I reply.

And I really mean it this time. I know it can't be easy for him to have that so messy. He's a clean freak. Him ignoring it for a while means that he cares.

"Okay, here it is," he places a map on his desk. They have two main houses on the property and one smaller house."

The map shows two big houses and a smaller one. There is a lot of clear space, probably where it's just grass.

"It's surrounded by woods," Noah says.

"Yes, which can be an advantage. It doesn't look like they have any cameras in the woods or people who patrol there," Phantom says.

"Odd."

My thoughts exactly. Why aren't they patrolling there? If I was the head of security there, I would either put up cameras, have people patrol every hour, or do both.

"Very odd. I looked into it, and this is only a small part of the Italian Mafia. Most of them are back in Italy," Phantom says.

That makes more sense, now. I don't think the actual Mafia Don would be that stupid to not have better security for the woods. The person who must be in charge here is an idiot.

"One of the main houses is close to the smaller building. The other main house is a mile away," Phantom says.

Looking closer at the map, I realize there are several dots and stars scattered across it. There are also times written on the map as well.

"What about the guards? When are they the weakest?" I ask.

I just want to get straight to the point. I want to know everything Phantom has so I can figure a way to get Marcy back.

"They have a couple times a day where they are weak. The

guards at night don't do much. They have never gotten attacked and so they have gotten more relaxed," Phantom says. "The other is when they are doing guard changes. There is a five-minute period where it's completely clear."

"You got all this information from Dom?" I ask.

Phantom nods his head.

"Good," Noah says. "We can just blast in there and kill them all."

"No," I reply, looking at Noah.

"Why?" he sits up straighter.

"Because, we want to rescue Marcy and leave it be. We don't want the Italian Mafia to come after us and slaughter us all. What good would that do us?"

"We can't just let them live! Who knows what they have done to Marcy!"

I take a deep breath in, trying to keep my cool. Noah obviously isn't thinking about the bigger picture and only his love for my daughter.

"Think of the bigger picture. We have blackmail on them from all the years Dom was working for them. We can get Marcy and Dom out and blackmail them. Tell them to leave us alone and we won't show any evidence to another mafia that wants to take them out," Phantom says. "Then they won't mess with our other charters anymore or we'll go public with this information."

Noah takes in some breaths, trying to calm down. You can see how livid he is that we are saying this. He just wants to go kill them all and doesn't think about the consequences.

"If you are going to disobey, and go kill everyone when we go there, we will lock your ass up here," I threaten.

He glares at me, not liking what I am saying.

"Do you understand me?" I ask. "Or do I just need to chain you to your bed now so you don't do anything fucking stupid?"

He continues to glare at me, but I can see him thinking through his options.

"Don't think he won't do it. I've seen him do it before," Phantom says, shuddering at the memory.

The guy was kicking and screaming the whole way. Even though he was a brother, I had to do it or else he would have killed us all.

He nods his head, acknowledging what I said.

"Not the fucking nod of the head. I want to hear you say you understand me and won't do it," I angrily say.

"Yes, I understand and won't do it," he says.

I turn my body towards Phantom.

"Okay, so do you have a plan on what we are going to do, or do I need to look more closely at the map and think of something?" I ask.

"I have a general idea. They are held in this house right here in cells. There are two guards who watch this house at the entrance. The main house is about one hundred meters away," Phantom explains, pointing to spots on the map.

"Great. And there are two guards at each entrance of the other house?" I ask, noticing the two dots at each door.

"Yes, but towards the night, they get relaxed and most of them head inside. Dom said there is normally one guard over here at this entrance. It isn't close enough to hear anything if we just go to where they are being held and grab them," Phantom goes on and explains.

"Great. How many men do we need for this?"

"I want a lot in case something goes wrong. Only six people will go get the girls but, we'll have several people in the trees waiting for our signal if things go wrong."

"Why the fuck do you keep saying them and the girls? It's only Marcy," Noah says.

I stare at Phantom, waiting for him to explain. I had heard him say that several times, but didn't think anything of it.

"Fuck. I forgot to tell you. There is another girl there with Marcy. She's apparently been there her whole life, and Marcy said she wouldn't leave without her. We're rescuing her too," Phantom says.

"Does that put Marcy in danger? That's a whole nother person," Noah asks.

"No, it won't put Marcy in any more danger than she already is in. If it was just Marcy, I would have sent three or four people."

I can see some tension leave Noah's body with that news. Another girl with Marcy? That's going to be interesting. Maybe we can leave the girl somewhere else, or maybe she has family. I groan when I realize that I doubt Marcy will let us just abandon the girl.

Jillian would also be the same. She would probably try to act like her mother.

"I've gotten permission from Pres to call the other MC in Arizona if we can use some of their men as backup. I haven't contacted them yet," Phantom says.

"Great. So, just an easy extraction. We've done a lot harder. We go in from the back and take out the guys guarding. Get the girls and leave," Noah says.

"What about the cameras? Can you hack into their system?" I ask.

"Yeah, I've been working on that and have figured a way to put it on a loop. They don't have many cameras, but the ones they do have I'll be able to cover our tracks," Phantom replies.

I nod my head and look back down at the map. This is going to work and I'm going to get my daughter back.

I try to come up with different scenarios that could happen.

Where could they hide people? Where could they ambush us if they find out we're coming? Is there a safe place to find cover?

I hear someone's phone ping, but I don't pay any attention to it. I don't want anything to go wrong while we are getting my daughter and the other girl back.

"Fuck," Phantom says.

I look up at Phantom really quick. His eyes are wide as he looks at me. What could be wrong?

CHAPTER SIXTEEN

MARCY

"Open the fucking cell!" someone yells.

I open my eyes, blinking several times to get the blurry vision away, and watch Mr. Rossi storming down the stairs.

Estella and I look at each other, panic and fear spread across our faces. His face is angry, his body tense as he walks towards us. This is different from all the other times he's come down here. When he came down here angry, it was him just being angry.

This time, Mr. Rossi is livid.

Fucking livid, and I had no clue what to do.

I've only had one person come in here as mad as Mr. Rossi is right now, and it didn't end well. I got beat to the brink of death. I couldn't move for three days. Estella told me the doctor came several times a day to make sure I was okay and healing well.

I don't remember any of it.

I don't remember that whole week.

The doctor came ten days after it happened and explained that I got hit in the head several times. Apparently making me not remember anything for a while. The doc doesn't know if I will ever get that memory back.

I don't know if I want those memories back. I wish I could forget everything that has happened here. It would make life easier.

So much easier.

I watch as the guard opens the cell right as Mr. Rossi gets to him. He stalks into the cell, straight towards me, but Estella steps in the way.

My eyes go wide. What the hell is she doing?

Mr. Rossi growls at her. Estella takes a step back, her body shaking in fear. Mr. Rossi's arm shoots out and pushes her.

Estella hits her head against the bars really hard. I flinch when she falls to the ground, her body still.

Mr. Rossi takes one step towards me and raises his clenched fist. Bringing it down, it connects with my jaw.

Pain erupts across my jaw. I groan in pain. So much pain.

"You fucking bitch!" he yells in my face.

Mr. Rossi grabs a fist full of my hair, yanking my head to stare him in the eyes. What have I done to warrant this behavior from him?

"You fucked him!" he accuses me.

Who did I fuck? I haven't fucked anyone; I've only gotten raped. I try to remember who raped me last. There have been so many guys that all their faces blur together and I can't tell them apart.

"Not only did one of my shipments and men get burnt, but you also fucked Rio! Spent hours with him." He slams my head against the wall.

Stars appear in my vision as I let out a groan in pain. A headache starts to form where he is holding my hair and slamming my head against the wall.

I try to remember who Rio is. Not many guards tell me their

names, most don't, but on very rare occasions one or two do. The past couple of days are a blur as I try to remember what happened. Rio. Who is Rio?

It dawned on me. Rio is Dom. Why would Mr. Rossi care if Dom fucked me or not? He obviously didn't, but he doesn't know that.

"The one person I was trying to keep you away from and you decide to fuck him." He spits on me.

I open my mouth to say something, but before I could, he slams my head against the wall again. I can feel blood running down my face.

His hands let go of my hair and I crumble to the floor. My whole body is shaking in fear. Mr. Rossi has never been this angry before and it terrifies me. I thought he was bad before, but this is even worse.

"You just can't keep your tight little cunt away from people. You little slut," he yells, kicking me in the stomach.

I curl in on myself, trying to protect my head and stomach. My arms protect my head while I bring my legs up to my chest.

Mr. Rossi bends down next to me. "Tell me. Did you enjoy it when he fucked you?"

I stay silent, not wanting to provoke him. There's nothing I can say. He didn't fuck me, but he doesn't know that.

"Tell me!" He kicks my shins.

I groan in pain as it starts throbbing.

"N-no," I whisper.

"No, what?" he asks.

"No, I didn't like it."

"That's right. You only like my cock in you. The way you get all tight and suck me in."

I whimper in pain and fear. That must have angered him.

"You stupid little bitch!" He stomps on my side.

The air is knocked out of me, and a snapping sound echos in the room. I scream in pain as tears stream down my face.

"Oh, such a satisfying sound," he says.

I move one of my hands as I hold my side. I can feel where my rib broke in half.

Mr. Rossi takes this advantage and kicks my head several times. Everything starts to get blurry and I can't think as straight.

I groan in pain and discomfort. Everything is moving when I look around the room. Moving and blurry and it's making me sick. I close my eyes when I feel bile rising in my throat.

"We're going to have so much fun," Mr. Rossi whispers in my ear. "We have an audience this time."

I'm hearing what he says, but not understanding a lick of it.

"Let's put on a show for them," he says.

Hands grip my stomach, hoisting me up onto my knees. My face is on the ground with my ass up. I feel dizzy and can't think straight.

What is Mr. Rossi doing?

"I'm gonna fuck you so hard. Maybe I'll fuck your ass too," he growls, ripping my pants and underwear.

My mind is dazed, hearing his words but not comprehending them.

I feel Mr. Rossi push my legs a little farther apart.

"Please, don't," I beg, realizing what is about to happen.

"You can beg all you want, but I'm not going to stop," he says.

Without warning, Mr. Rossi slams into me. I scream, the burning sensation taking over my body. I feel like I am being ripped apart.

He starts to grunt as he pulls out and thrusts back in. His hand circles around me, rubbing my clit super hard.

"Please stop," I beg, pain lacing my voice.

He continues to slam into me. He grabs my hips and pulls me backwards as he rams forward. All I can feel is pain from the force he uses.

I turn my head and bite my arm. I try to distract myself from the pain, so I look over at Estella, trying to see if she is okay. Her back is against the bar cells. She looks dazed, but I can see that she is coming to her senses.

Her eyes go wide as she sees Mr. Rossi rape me in front of her. She tries to move, determination in her eyes to come save me.

I make eye contact with her and shake my head. If she interferes, everything is going to get worse. For the both of us.

Mr. Rossi is furious this time, and I'm worried that if she tries to stop him that she'll get killed. I don't think I can handle someone else dying in front of me.

Bile rises in my throat thinking about the doctor being killed in front of us. The life leaving his eyes. Pool of blood forming around him as he bled out. His blood on us.

She stares into my eyes, trying to figure out what I'm telling her. I mouth the word 'no' to her, wincing as Mr. Rossi grips my hips really hard.

Estella winces as she watches Mr. Rossi brutally rape me. She leans up against the bars and closes her eyes.

I look down at the ground, trying to think of anything other than him being in me. How am I ever going to tell my parents that I was raped? How am I going to tell Noah that he won't take my virginity? That I've been tainted and used by men for the past two months.

I groan as everything starts to ache more as he rams into me. I can feel the pressure building up in my stomach as he rubs my clit. I can feel myself wanting a release.

Tears appear in my eyes as I feel myself clench around him. As much as I hate this, my body loves it. I feel myself getting closer to release and I try everything to stop myself from cumming.

I'm disgusted with myself for this. Who gets raped and has an orgasm?

My mind never believes that I'm about to orgasm. Mr. Rossi tilts his hips slightly, making his dick go in deeper. The pressure reaches its peak and I feel myself come around him.

"Such a dirty little slut. Look at you cumming for me like a good little slut you are," he says, pulling out of me.

His fingers plunge into me, coating them with my juices.

"I think I'll take your ass now," he says, trailing his fingers towards my ring.

He lightly runs his fingers around my ring. My body stills and I try to move, but his other hand grips my hips.

"You're going to take this like a dirty slut you are." He plunges one of his fingers into me.

There is a burning sensation at my ring where he forces two of his fingers into me. I cry out, all the discomfort at the front of my mind.

His fingers move out of me, and I sigh in relief. I should have known that he was going to put them back in.

He plunges his fingers back into my ass, moving them around. I groan in pain as he scissor cuts inside me.

"So tight," he growls. "I think you're ready."

Before I can shout, his fingers get pulled out and are replaced by the head of his cock. He moans as he pushes into me.

A burning sensation appears at my ring as he pushes into me.

"Fuck. Your ass is so tight around my cock. I'm not going to last long," he grunts, pushing the rest of himself into me.

Tears stream down my face as he slowly moves in and out of me. It hurts so bad. He forced his semi-wet dick into my ass.

His thrusts are slow but hard, prolonging the pain. I bite my arm, trying to block the pain he is inflicting on me.

My left side burns and aches, as I take in a deep, shaky breath. My broken rib is hurting and making it difficult to breath.

"I'm so close," he says, ramming into me.

I feel his dick start to twitch as he gets closer to his release. He almost pulls all the way out before sliding right back in. Moaning, he picks up the pace as he chases his release. His thrusts become more chaotic the closer he gets.

He stills his movements as I feel him fill me up with him cum. He leans forward, placing one of his hands on my back.

"So good," he mumbles.

Mr. Rossi spits on me as he pulls out of me. Once he's completely out, I feel myself fall over on the ground.

"Lock up," Mr. Rossi says. "And tell the boys her ass is great for a fuck."

I hear his footsteps leave as the door shuts. The clinking sound of the cell door being locked has Estella shakily moving across the room. I watch her, but don't move.

"I'm so sorry," Estella hoarsely says. "You don't deserve any of this."

Estella sits down and gently helps me move. My head is placed on her lap.

"You're going to be alright," she whispers, running her hands through my hair.

Tears fill my eyes as I think about what just happened. This has been by far the most brutal raping yet. He showed no mercy.

Everything comes crashing down on me. Sobs wrack my body as everything plays in my mind.

"Shhh, it's going to be okay," Estella whispers, stroking my hair.

"I, I orgasmed," I say, sobbing. "How could I do that? I hated every minute of it."

"Shhh, it's okay. It's just your body reacting. That doesn't mean you wanted it or didn't hate it. We can't help that our bodies react to that," Estella tells me.

"I'm disgusted with myself. I don't remember ever doing that any other time."

Estella stops her movements and grabs my face.

I turn my face, and we make eye contact. "That's because you were numb. You were in a daze."

More tears appear in my eyes. I just want to die. Die and not have to relive any of this.

"It's going to be okay. You get some rest now. I'll watch over you," she whispers.

I nod my head and turn my head on her lap. I close my eyes tight. Maybe a little rest will help me calm down some.

CHAPTER SEVENTEEN

BEAR

"What?" I ask.

"Two days," Phantom says in disbelief.

"Two days till what?"

My patience is wearing thin.

"Until fight," he says, looking back down at his phone.

"Speak in a fucking full sentence," I growl.

"We have two days until the Italian Mafia will be its weakest. Something has happened. Dom said to get all of our men ready and head to Arizona."

Two days until I get my daughter back? I can't fucking believe it. I thought I was going to have to wait a whole month or more until we could get her.

"Do you know what happened?" Noah asks.

"Someone burned a shipment and men of theirs," Phantom replies.

"Alive?"

My head turns to Noah. Why the fuck does he want to know if they were alive?

"Probably," Phantom says, typing on his phone.

"Do we know who burned their shipment and men?" I ask.

Maybe this could be good for us.

"I don't, but I'm going to look and see if I can figure it out. Why?" Phantom says, turning his computer on.

"It could be good for us," I reply.

"Care to elaborate." Phantom gives me a look.

I let out a little chuckle. Of course he would want me to explain. "Well, whoever did it could have their attention for a while. Maybe they'll think that the group took the girls. Could get the Italian Mafia off our backs until they figure it out."

"Fucking genius," Phantom says, shaking his head.

I crack a smile. I normally keep everything to myself unless it's super important or can help. I think through everything before I say it. That's gotten me the reputation of being a genius, apparently. I'm not, but the guys think I am.

"Find out who did it while I call the Pres of the other club," I say.

Phantom nods and starts typing on his computer. I open my phone before I realize that I need the other Pres's phone number.

"Do we need to run it by my dad first?" Noah speaks up.

"Wouldn't hurt," Phantom says. "I've already talked to him about this before."

Right, my head is anywhere but where it needs to be. My thoughts are all over the place. I can't believe I'm getting my daughter back, but at the same time I'm worried about leaving Jillian here when I leave.

"Call the Pres, real quick, before we call the other MC. Get his approval," Phantom says.

"You don't have to fucking tell me. I'm not stupid," I grumble. "You also can fucking call him."

I take my phone out of my pocket and call Pres.

"What's up, Bear," Pres says.

"Hey, I can fill you in later, but is it okay to call the other MC in Arizona and have them help get my daughter back?" I ask.

"Yeah, that's fine. Phantom filled me in before, but I think you have new information. The other MC knows we may need their help," he says. "You call them and we'll all be waiting in the room for church."

"Thanks," I hang up the phone.

I look up at Phantom as he types on his computer.

"We got the clear. I need the President's phone number for the other MC. After we call them, we have church," I say, filling in Phantom and Noah.

They both nod. Phantom hands me a piece of paper with a phone number on it.

"That's the Pres's number for the other MC," he says. "Put it on speaker when you call."

I nod my head and put the phone number in. I turn it on speaker before placing it on the table. The phone rings several times before someone finally picks up.

"Hello?" a deep voice fills the room.

Tank is the other MC's President. Great guy and massive. You would think he is tough, but if you see him around his kids and wife, you realize he isn't all that tough.

"Hey, it's Bear from Hell's Reaper," I say.

"Bear, how have you been holding up? I heard your daughter got taken two, almost three months ago. Sorry to hear that."

"Thanks man. It's been fucking rough."

Silence fills the room. Noah starts chuckling but quickly stops when Phantom smacks him behind the head. It's no laughing matter.

"Sorry," he whispers.

"So, why have you called me?" Tank asks.

"It's actually related to my daughter. We've already got the okay from our Pres to call and ask you. We're going in to get her in two days. Wondering if you'd give us backup," I say.

"Yeah! Come by the clubhouse. Give us a rundown, and we'll help out any way we can."

"Thanks, brother. We'll see you either late tonight or tomorrow."

He hangs up, and I let out a sigh of relief. I never have to worry if Tank has our backs, but there is always that feeling they may not.

"Alright, let's go to church," I say, standing up from my chair.

I don't wait for the other two as I make my way towards our church room. Once I make it to the room, I take my seat two seats down from our Pres, Noah and Phantom following close behind.

"Alright, now that all of us are here we have some business to discuss," Pres says.

Everyone stares at him. I wonder who he wants to speak and explain everything.

"Bear, you can explain everything," he says.

All eyes turn to me.

"I'm just cutting straight to the point. Phantom gathered all the information, so he gets all the credit," I start off. "We have a chance in two days to get my daughter and another girl back."

Everyone hollers and cheers when I say this. I lift my hand, quieting the whole room.

"Quiet!" I yell when they don't.

Everyone falls silent.

"She got taken by the Italian Mafia. Apparently, Jillian's ex-boyfriend was working for them, and they didn't like that we killed him. Good news is we have an inside source in the Italian Mafia."

"What's the plan?" Gears asks.

Phantom places a big map of the compound on the table.

"They have three buildings on the property and a lot of fucking open fields surrounding it. One of the big main buildings is off, so we don't have to worry about that. The smaller building is where the girls are being held. The big building is the main building," I say, pointing to the spots on the map as I speak.

"Girls?" Butch asks.

"Yeah, there is another girl with Marcy. Apparently, she's been there her whole life and Marcy said she wouldn't leave without her," I say. "So, that means things may change around here for a little while because she doesn't know how we live. Hasn't been around nice people."

"Understand?" Pres says.

"Yes," everyone replies.

"Just treat her like you would my wife or daughter. Any old lady. With respect and softness. Especially soft. No raised voices around her until we know what she can handle," I say.

Everyone nods their heads with understanding. I hope the girl isn't that damaged, but being with the Italian Mafia her whole life, she probably will be. It's going to take a special someone to help her out and to love her.

"We are attacking at night. That's when their guards are lazy," Phantom says.

"The guards are lazy? It's the fucking mafia." Gears laughs.

"It's a smaller group of the Italian Mafia," I reply. "Not concerned about much, it doesn't seem."

"Fucking right. Who has guards that are fucking lazy? That's one way to get attacked."

And I completely agree with him. I don't know what the

head of this smaller group is thinking, but he clearly isn't thinking much. You never leave yourself vulnerable. You never let your guards get lazy.

"A team of six is going to go grab the girls. I was thinking Butch, Gears, Whiskey, Phantom, Stitch, and myself will go and get the girls. Everyone else will be staying in the woods waiting for our signal if we need help," I say.

"No!" Noah says, gaining everyone's attention.

My back straightens, and I look at him. "What's wrong?"

"I want to be part of the six. Marcy is my girl, and I should be there," he says.

"Will you be able to fucking control yourself and not go off and kill everyone?"

He glares at me, but I glare right back.

"If you fucking can't do that, then you can't be one of the six. We aren't there to kill everyone. Just the two guards that are guarding the small building," I say.

It's silent and I take that as a no. I look back at the map.

"I can. You just have to let me be one of the six. I need to make sure she is okay," Noah speaks up.

"Okay, you'll take Stitch's place," I say, looking at him.

He nods his head and leans back in his chair.

"Okay, now that we have that out of the way, we are hoping that it will be an easy in and out. You all need to be ready to help us if we need it," I say, looking at everyone in the room. "I'm also thinking of leaving Ink and Hacker here in case something happens."

Everyone nods their head. Great. I sit back in my seat and look at Phantom. About time he started speaking instead of me.

"We called the MC that's in Arizona for backup and they agreed. We also have an advantage," Phantom says.

"What kind of advantage?" Gears asks.

"Apparently, the American Mafia didn't like that the Italian

Mafia is here, so they burned one of their shipments and men down the other day. Our source said the leader is sending a lot of the men to attack them."

"Great!" Butch says with a smile.

Everyone goes silent when we don't have any more information.

"It's about a seven-hour drive to the other MC's clubhouse. We'll take a vote to see if we leave tonight or tomorrow morning," Pres says. "All in favor of leaving tonight raise your hand."

All but three raise their hand, two of them being Ink and Hacker.

"Majority rules. We leave tonight. Go spend time with your significant others before we leave," Pres says. "We leave in an hour. Church dismissed."

I push my chair back and leave the room, heading straight towards mine.

"Where have you been?" Jillian asks when I walk into the room.

"Talking to Phantom. I just got out of church," I say, sitting on the bed.

Jillian lays her head on my lap.

"Everything okay?" she asks.

"Yeah, everyone but Ink and Hacker and leaving tonight for Arizona. We are going to get Marcy in two days, but it's a seven-hour drive and we need to get prepared," I run my hands through her hair.

Her body stills.

"Your leaving?" she whispers.

"I know, baby. I don't want to leave, but I want to get Marcy back. I'll be back by the end of the week. You won't even realize I'm gone."

I really fucking hate leaving her. Especially when she is

pregnant. It kills me inside, but I know I need to do this. I need to be there when we get Marcy back.

"It's going to feel like a year," she says. "But you get our girl!"

"Ink and Hacker will keep you entertained."

She lets out a sigh and sits up. Tears are in her eyes, but none have fallen.

"Don't cry. Everything is going to be okay. We're getting Marcy back," I whisper, grabbing her face in my hands.

I lean forward and kiss her lips.

"I need to pack something light and get ready. I leave in less than thirty minutes." I stand up from the bed.

Jillian watches me as I pack up a few essentials into my backpack.

"Do you want to stay in here or come downstairs with me?" I ask.

"Down with you." She pulls the covers back and slides out of the bed.

Jillian walks over to me and wraps her arms around my waist. We walk out of my room and down the stairs in this position.

"Look who finally decided to show up," Butch hollers.

"I still have fucking five minutes," I growl.

I start to get annoyed at Butch. He doesn't have an old lady, so he doesn't know what it feels like to say goodbye to them. To have to leave them and know that you may not come back alive. Someday, and I hope soon, he finds a girl he can ask to be his old lady, so he knows how it fucking feels. So, he won't be hollering to get going when you still have fucking five minutes left.

Everyone laughs and goes back to what they're doing. Jillian and I walk outside and towards my bike. Placing my bag down on the ground, I bring Jillian into me. It's hard hugging a pregnant woman, but I do my best not to hurt her.

"Everything is going to be okay," I whisper into her ear. "I'll be back before you know it."

I pull back, kiss Jillian on the lips, and slide onto my bike. Tears glisten in her eyes and it takes everything in me to not go back to her and never leave.

Pulling my helmet on, I turn my bike on and follow Pres away from the club.

CHAPTER EIGHTEEN

MARCY

Sleep never came to me. I tried and tried to fall asleep, to forget everything that had just happened, but I couldn't. I feel dirty and numb.

I want so hard to cry and let everything out, but my eyes won't tear up. My whole body is numb, emotionally and physically.

"Everything is going to be okay," Estella whispers to me.

We've been sitting here for who knows how long. Estella running her hands through my hair, and I stare off into the distance, unfocused.

My eyes won't focus on anything. It's like my eyes and brain have shut off, wanting to retreat on themselves.

For a long time, I felt Mr. Rossi's cum trail out of my ass and onto my thighs. It felt so uncomfortable, but Estella told me that I needed to let it come all out.

I wanted to cry so bad, in that instance. I felt so dirty and violated, but my body wouldn't cry. Not a single tear came out of my eyes. I thought for a second that I may be broken, and I think Estella knew what I was thinking. She told me I was in shock and that it would come crashing down at some point.

Who knows when that time would be?

I was worried when it would happen. What if we were cleaning and all the sudden, I broke down? We are told not to cry, or we will get punishments. I don't want another punishment after what I just received.

Some guards are more lenient on crying. A few of them like it when you cry, it turns them on. Several guards that like it know how to make me or Estella cry. How they can push us to make us break down.

"Let us through! Boss said we needed to check up on the girls," a voice yells.

My body tenses up, not liking the sound of them. Maybe the new doctor is coming to see me, and the damage Mr. Rossi inflicted on me. I wouldn't be surprised if I had a couple of tears from how hard he thrusted into me.

Estella and I hear the door open, and we stay in our spots. Every doctor we've had always tells us to not move, which shocks us. We thought they would want the same respect everyone else gets. Us standing in position for them.

Three sets of footsteps are heard walking towards our cell, confirming that the doctor is with them. I feel my body relax a little. Anytime the doctor has come to us, it's always been him and two guards.

I look at the cell door, waiting for them to show up. Three faces appear with wicked smiles on their face and no doctor. I flinch as the guard opens the door and all three of them stalk into the cell.

I bring my head off of Estella's lap and watch them come towards us. What are they doing here? It can't be time for any of them to play with us. This is so out of schedule. It hasn't been a long time since Mr. Rossi was here.

"Look, you can see the fear in their eyes," one guy says.

All three of them laugh.

"One of them doesn't have to be afraid if she stays out of our way," another one says.

I suck in a breath. Who's going to take on these three guys? I don't want it to be me, but at the same time I don't want it to be Estella. Taking three guys is hard and so much pain is involved. I wish they wouldn't be here at all, but I can't stop them.

Estella and I couldn't stop them together even if we tried. We are frail and weak while they are muscular and taller than us. There's also one more of them than us, which gives them another advantage.

"Frank, what do you think we should do to the girl?" the first guy asks.

Frank takes a step forward and looks at both of us, not giving away who is going to be picked.

"I think one person should take her pussy, another her mouth, and the third has her ass," Frank speaks up. "Maybe we can have turns in each spot."

I know all the color drains from my face. Whenever I've had multiple guys in the room, they have taken turns, or one takes my pussy while the other takes my mouth. Never have I had all three of them doing something, and it scares me.

"I think we should have the other girl watch the whole thing," the third guy speaks.

"Good thinking, Miguel," the first guy says.

All of them look at each other and grin wickedly. I take in a shaky breath, scared for our lives. I hope whoever gets the guys makes it. I've heard that this Frank guy is brutal. He doesn't show mercy to anyone.

"Well, Frank. Go get our girl for the night," Miguel says.

Frank takes a step forward, making Estella and I lean back. I try to look around to find a way out of this, but the other two guys position themselves, so we don't have anywhere to go. I watch as Frank takes a step closer to me and my heart sinks to my feet.

No.

This can't be happening.

Mr. Rossi just finished with me like an hour ago. I can't take three men.

"Please, don't do this," I whisper.

Frank steps right in front of me and bends down.

"Too bad. Mr. Rossi said we can have you all to ourselves. Do whatever we want for however long we want," he whispers in my ear.

His hand shoots out, wrapping his hand around my neck. He squeezes and my eyes water. My lungs are begging me for air the longer he has his hold on my throat.

"We want her alive while we fuck her," Miguel says.

Frank lets me go and I gasp for air. My lungs burn from not having air in them. I watch as Frank grabs Estella's arm and yanks her across the room.

Miguel steps closer to me, a grin on his face.

"Oh, the things I'm going to do to you." He closes his eyes and moans.

I want to throw up, as I watch his dick grow in his pants. He stuffs his hands down his pants and starts to palm himself.

The other guy takes a step towards me and grabs my hands. He yanks me up to my feet and before I can register what he's doing, all my clothes are ripped and on the floor.

"I want to take her pussy first," Miguel says, taking his hand out of his pants.

"I'll take her ass," the other guy says. "Lay on the ground."

Miguel takes his clothes off and lays them on the ground, laying on them. The other guy pushes me forward and I stumble.

I look down and Miguel grins at me. I feel hands on me,

pushing me down. Without warning, I feel Miguel enter me, making me scream out in pain.

It feels like sandpaper as he moves in and out of me. Tears spring to my eyes and I choke on a sob. So much pain.

Frank and the other guy start to take their clothes off as they watch Miguel thrust into me. They both start to run their hands up and down their dicks, getting off on Miguel raping me.

Out of the corner of my eyes, I see Estella move from her spot. Before I can tell her not to do anything, she runs into Frank, but he doesn't move.

Her eyes go wide. Frank lets his dick go and turns around with a furious face. He pushes her, making her fly as she hits her head on the bars.

"Stop. Please. Take me instead of her," she begs.

Frank stalks towards her, purpose in his footsteps. Miguel starts to harshly rub my clit, making me hiss in pain.

"I'll do anything you want. Just please take me," Estella whispers.

"Shut up, bitch," Frank yells at Estella.

Miguel continues to thrust into my pussy as I watch Frank punch Estella and tie her up. The third guy pulls my ass cheeks apart and spits on me. Tears stream down my face as I feel him start to enter my ass.

"Stop. Please," I beg.

My begging falls onto deaf ears. The guy continues to push himself into me.

The spit didn't do anything to help the guy start to enter me. The burning sensation intensifies the further he pushes into me.

"Miguel, stop thrusting into her so I can enter her ass fully," the guy grunts.

"Hurry the fuck up, Pedro," Miguel stops his movements.

Pedro starts to push himself further into me. I feel myself getting tore in two the further he enters me.

"Stop. It hurts," I try to pull away from Pedro.

A hard slap comes down onto my ass, making me yelp in pain.

"Shut the fuck up and stay still," Pedro says.

Hands land on my hips and hold me in place. Pedro stops moving and I feel so uncomfortable and full.

"Can I start moving?" Miguel asks.

"Yeah," Pedro grunts.

I try and relax my body, so it won't hurt as much, but it won't. I have two objects in me that I don't want. That they forced into me.

Miguel starts moving first, not fully pulling out of me. As Miguel thrusts into me, Pedro pulls out. They go opposite of each other. I keep making incoherent sounds, most of them from pain.

Everything hurts as they continue to thrust in and out of me.

"Fuck. This feels fucking amazing," Miguel grunts as he thrusts into me.

"So tight. Boss was right," Pedro says.

Both of them pick up their pace. They thrust in harder, moving my whole body. My legs feel weak, and I feel like I am going to fall down any second. Miguel's grip tightens on my hips, trying to keep me in place.

"Stop," I beg.

I don't want this.

"Please," I say.

They continue to thrust into me. Tears blur my vision.

"Stop. Please. I'm begging you," I raise my voice.

"Frank. Just shut the bitch up," Miguel yells.

I blink several times, trying to figure out where Frank is. He's the worst of them all. He shows no mercy when he fucks girls.

I watch a figure start to walk towards me. I open my mouth, but he grips my jaw with his hands.

"Hmm, how should I shut you up?" he whispers in my ear.

I try to close my mouth, but his grip doesn't let me. His other hand moves towards his pants, unbuckling them.

My eyes go wide when I realize what he's about to do. I try to move back, but Miguel and Pedro's thrusts keep me in place.

Frank lets his hard dick free from its confinements.

"You're going to take this like the dirty little slut you are," he says.

Without warning, he thrusts his dick into my mouth, choking me. I gag when he hits the back of my throat.

"Don't you dare throw up!" he yells.

I try to think of other things. I don't know what he'll do if I throw up, but I don't want to find out.

My teeth slightly graze his cock, making him hiss. Frank pulls out of my mouth and slaps me on the face. If Miguel's hands weren't tightly on my hips, I would have fallen over.

"No fucking teeth!" he yells in my face.

Frank pries my mouth open and thrusts his cock into my mouth right as Miguel and Pedro thrust into me. My scream gets drowned out by Frank's dick in my mouth.

Tears stream down my face as all three of them brutally thrust into me. Slobber runs down my chin and onto Miguel below me. All three of them are grunting as they get closer to their releases.

I can feel myself start choking on Frank's dick. My lungs want air in them, but it's hard when his cock keeps hitting the back of my throat. He pulls out slightly, letting me take a breath of air before thrusting back in.

All three of them thrust at the same time, making me see stars in my eyes. Pain radiates everywhere in my body. With each thrust comes a sharp pain and more tears streaming down my face.

"I'm close," Miguel says, his thrusts become faster.

"Me too," Pedro says.

"Hollow out your cheeks! I'm close," Frank yells.

I try to hollow my cheeks out, but it's so hard with everything going on. Pedro slaps my ass really hard.

"He said hollow your cheeks," he grunts.

I hollow my cheeks more. All their movements become more chaotic the closer they get to their release. Another set of hands appear on my stomach, holding me up. My legs have given out at this point, but with Miguel and Pedro's hold, they are keeping me upright.

Without warning, all three of them pull out of me. Pedro lets go of me and stands up fully. Miguel pushes me to the side, making me land on my side really hard. I let out a cry, feeling my arm twist in a painful way.

Miguel stands up and all three of them huddle next to each other, standing right in front of me. I try to sit up, but my body is exhausted and in pain.

All three of them start to jack off, their movements fast. I have no energy to move when I realize what they are about to do. Miguel is the first to cum, all of it hitting me in the stomach. Frank is next, his cum landing all over my face and hair. Pedro is last, his release spraying me on the legs.

More tears stream down my face.

"Look at our masterpiece," Frank says.

"Fucking masterpiece," Miguel says.

They all start to get dressed quickly, Frank releasing Estella from her bounds, and then they make their way towards the cell door.

"No cleaning up for you," Pedro says, shutting the door. "If you do, you'll get a worse punishment. I want all the cum to dry on you."

I feel so humiliated with their cum on me. Estella comes over towards me, putting my head on her lap.

"Shhh, I'm so sorry that happened to you," she whispers.

She runs her hand through my hair, and I watch as she grimaces when she touches Frank's cum. I want to puke, cry, and die all at once.

I feel so drained. So numb, the longer I lay my head in her lap. I don't know what to do. How to process everything that just happened to me.

I honestly don't want to process everything that just happened. I want to forget it ever happened. I want to pretend it never happened and go on with my life.

Estella and I stay in this position until I succumb to the darkness.

CHAPTER NINETEEN

NOAH

After a long seven hours of driving, we finally made it to the other MC compound. It's significantly smaller than ours, but they've always been there for us when we needed it and we've been there for them as well.

The seven-hour long drive gave me a lot of time to think. I knew that Dom was our informant for the past couple of years. I had questioned my dad, because I had remembered him, but didn't know where he went. Finally, my dad told me that he was there.

My dad, a couple of days ago, came to me and told me that they figured out where Marcy was, and that Dom was with her. I didn't know any details besides that, and I told my dad I wanted to send a message to her. I hope she got it, and knew I was coming for her.

Currently, my dad, Bear, Gears, and Butch are talking to the other MC, filling them in on everything that is going down. I'm in the room with them but am hardly paying attention. The only thing on my mind is getting Marcy back.

I'll do fucking anything for her. I'm prepared to kill anyone and everyone to get her back.

"We're leaving in a couple of hours to go get the girls," my dad says.

"What can we do for you?" the other president asks.

"Just backup. Stay in the woods and if we need you, we'll either give a signal or you'll know when to come," Bear says.

My mind wanders back to Marcy. What could they have done to her the past two almost three months? Is she okay? Has she been fed properly?

I have no doubt she was probably treated like trash, and it breaks my heart to think about that. She should be treated like a fucking queen. Pampered and spoiled, but here she is being a prisoner with who knows what, happening to her.

I try to keep my mind away from what could have happened to her. I don't know if I ever want to know, but at the same time I do, so I can go after and kill the fuckers who did this to her.

I know I promised Bear that I wouldn't go after them, this time. Doesn't mean I won't go after them later. I'm going to make it my mission to go after everyone who has hurt her and kill them. I don't care about the consequences, I just want to avenge what happened to Marcy.

Marcy has me wrapped around her finger. I would do anything and everything for her. I don't know if she knows that, but I'm going to make sure and let her know anything she wants done; I'll do it.

She won't go to any other man about this. She'll only come to me to get things done. She's mine, always has been, and I'm going to make sure she fucking knows it. Marcy isn't going to leave my sight when she comes back.

"I know that look," Butch says.

I look up at him and shake my head. He doesn't know this look.

"What look?" I reply.

He laughs. "The 'I'm going to murder everyone that stands in the way of my girl' look."

I stay silent. So what if he knows that look. Doesn't mean shit.

"Bear had the same look when Jillian was taken by her ex," Butch says. "He made sure Jillian wasn't out of his sight for months and months, even though her ex was dead."

I chuckle. That sounds like him. He has a possessive streak for Jillian. I've heard the story of him asking her out and how he got her to be his girlfriend.

"Word of advice. Show Marcy that you love her, but don't smother her and not let her breathe." Butch leans against the wall.

"What do you know about this?" I ask.

He doesn't have a girl. He's almost forty years old and I've never seen him around a girl.

"Because I made the mistake of smothering mine. Shit happened, and look where it brought me," he says. "No girl."

Shock fills my face. He had a girl? I wonder when that was. It would've had to be before I was born. I wonder why people have never brought it up, probably because it's a sore subject for him. I wonder what happened to the girl. Where did she go?

"Just promise me that you won't smother her. I would hate for anything to happen to her. And don't force her to tell you anything. You don't want to push her away from you," he says.

"Yeah, I promise," I reply.

It's all great advice. It seems like he knows what he's talking about.

"When we get her back, if you ever need to talk, don't hesitate to come to me. I don't want you to make the same mistakes I made," he says.

"Yeah, I will." I push myself off the wall.

It seems like everyone is finishing talking. Maybe we can go ahead and just leave for the other compound where the girls are being held.

A hand is placed on my shoulder, stopping me from walking away.

"Don't do anything stupid when we go and rescue the girls. You promised Bear you wouldn't do anything, and everyone is holding you to it. I know it's your girl, but we need you to have a clear head through all of this," Butch says.

"I promise. Clear head and I won't do anything stupid," I reply.

He drops his hands from my shoulder and walks towards the other guys. I follow him and wait for the guys to finish their conversation.

"It hasn't been a couple of hours, but our informant said they start getting lazy about now. By the time we get there, everything will be a go," Phantom says.

"Let me tell my guys while you get ready. We won't be long," the president says.

He and his men walk away, leaving the room. I hope he just gives a brief explanation since they won't be doing much, and we can get on our way.

"Let's head to our bikes and get ready. By the time we are done, they'll be done also and ready to go," my dad says.

Everyone files out of the room and towards our bikes. Nerves start running through my body, making me take a deep breath in. I need to stay calm and collected through everything, so I don't mess up.

I can't wait to get Marcy back and have everything go back to normal.

"Remember, us six are going in. We only kill the two guards in front of the building, and we do it quietly. Then we go and get the girls, leaving quickly," Bear says. "This MC is providing a van so the girls can sit on the way back."

"They are also bringing their doctor with them in case they need medical attention," Phantom says.

I hope they don't need medical attention, but a pit starts forming in my stomach. I have a feeling that they are going to need the doctor and that doesn't sit well with me.

"Are we bringing our van with us?" I ask.

"No, why would we?" Butch says.

"What if the doctor needs help? Where will the bikes go if some of the brothers ride with the doc?"

All of them stare at me, some turn into shock.

"I didn't think about that," Bear mutters.

He turns his body. "Pres!"

My dad walks towards us.

"What do you need?" he asks.

"Your son had a good idea. We need to bring our van in case some brothers need to ride with doc to help out. Put their bikes in the other van," Bear says.

A grin spreads across his face. "Great thinking, son. We'll bring our van."

I let out a sigh of relief. I don't know why, but it makes me feel better, but the pit is still in my stomach.

"I have a bad feeling about this," I say.

"What?" Butch asks.

Before I can say anything, the other president walks out of the building.

"We're ready," he yells.

Everyone gets on their bikes and turns them on. We wait for my dad's signal, letting us know we can leave.

"We ride," he yells, riding off.

* * *

We've been standing in the woods for a while now. Watching the guards to see if anything is going to change. I stare intently at the two guards at the front entrance.

I can't wait to get my fucking hands on them and kill them. I hope the guys let me kill one of them. I'll just have to make sure I get there before anyone else does.

"Can we go?" I ask impatiently.

"Wait," Bear says, shooting me a look.

I turn my head and my eyes go wide. Two guys are fast walking towards the building, wicked grins on their face. They say something to the guards and walk into the building.

The pit in my stomach grows more. I don't have a good feeling about them walking into the building at all. I need to get there now.

"Okay, the six of us move," Bear says.

All six of us get up and quietly make our way towards the building. I make sure I'm behind Bear, securing that I get a kill. We line ourselves against the buildings, so we have the element of surprise.

"Follow me," Bear whispers.

We make our way towards the front of the building. Bear turns around.

"I'll kill the first guy and you follow behind me and kill the second guy," he says.

I nod my head and follow him around the corner. The guards are standing several feet in front of the doors, paying attention to their phones. Such idiots.

Bear silently walks behind the first guy, and I make my way to the second. I bring my knife out and wait for Bear to start. Right as he grabs his guy, I wrap my hand on my guy's face, covering his mouth. I quickly bring the knife up and run it across his throat.

I keep my hands on his mouth for a couple of extra seconds,

just in case he makes any noise. Feeling his body lean up against mine, I let the guard hit the ground.

Turning to Bear, I watch as he lets his guy drop to the ground. He pulls his head around the corner and motions for the other guys to follow.

I honestly don't know why we need the other four, but Phantom was adamant about having six people in total.

I stand next to the door and try to listen in. I hear several screams and I turn towards the guys.

"Hurry the fuck up. The girls are screaming," I raise my voice.

They all look alarmed and rush towards me. I open the doors and rush down the stairs knife ready to strike. I take in the whole room, trying to figure out where they are. A stench of piss fills the room and I try hard not to throw up.

The building is full of different cells, all but one empty. I take the situation in and feel bile rise in my throat. Two males are trying to force themselves onto our girls.

My vision turns red as I run towards the cell, knife ready to kill those fuckers. Butch is close behind me. I take the first guy, pulling him by his collar towards me. Before he has time to even react fully, I plunge the knife into his chest and twist.

The man screams in pain and flails in my arms. I keep my firm grip on him and stab him again. I must have hit him in the lung because he starts gasping and making a gurgling sound, drowning in his own blood.

I drop his body to the ground and look over at Butch. His guy is dead, laying in his own pool of blood. I grin and nod my head. We've done good today.

I take in the cell, everything is dirty. Red stains on the ground, a bucket in the corner filled with piss and shit. I place my hand over my nose, breathing through my mouth so I don't have to smell this.

"Please, no," someone mumbles.

I look over and watch as Butch tries to talk to a girl I don't recognize. I move my eyes across the cell, trying to find Marcy. My eyes stop in the corner where Marcy is huddled and shaking, completely naked.

"Marcy?" I whisper.

Her eyes snap up and take me in. I search her eyes, but all I see are lifeless eyes, and that scares the shit out of me. What happened to her?

CHAPTER TWENTY

JILLIAN

Sobs wrack my body as I watch Bear leave the compound with the other guys. My heart breaks because I don't want anything to happen to him or any of the guys. I have this bad feeling that something terrible is going to happen and someone won't be coming home.

I feel my breathing quicken the farther he gets away. My airway starts to close, and I panic. My hand flies to my throat and I hold it.

Bear is going to come back in one piece with Marcy. Everyone is going to come back in one piece. No matter what I think, I still feel a pit in my stomach, and I can't stop my airway from closing even more.

The noise around me starts to get muffled the longer I can't breathe.

"Jillian?" a muffled voice says.

My head whips over towards the direction of the person, my eyes wide with panic. I open my mouth and try to take a breath in. I manage to get in a little breath, but that makes me panic even more.

Will my baby be alright? I don't want anything to happen to him or her.

My panic rises even more when I think about this.

Ink takes a step toward me and places his hands on my shoulders.

"Listen to my voice," he says.

His voice is a little clearer since he stepped closer to me, but it's still a little muffled.

I open my mouth again; panic shows on my face when I can't take a breath in this time. Ink grabs my free hand and places it on his chest. His other hand moves my face to keep it trained on his face.

"Follow my breathing," I read his mouth.

I feel his chest fill with air, and I try to follow him.

"Just pay attention to my breathing and my voice. Nothing else," he says.

My hearing is slowly coming back, and I shakily match his breathing. He takes slow breaths of air, letting me match it.

"That's it. You are doing amazing," he says, giving me a smile.

Once my breathing is back to normal, I look around and see Hacker looking at me with panic filled eyes. I feel exhausted, but I manage to give him a small smile.

"I think we should take you to the doc. Get you checked over just in case," Hacker says.

My eyes go wide. "There's no need. I'm just worried about everyone that left. I hope they all come back in one piece with my daughter."

"I agree with Hacker. I think we should go get you checked out. Just make sure you and the baby are okay. I would hate not to go and something goes wrong later," Ink says.

I let out a sigh. "Okay."

They both smile at me. Hacker and Ink stand right next to me as we walk back into the compound.

"I'll text the doc. He should be on the compound," Hacker says.

Ink helps me sit down on one of the couches. I sink into it and relax.

"Need anything?" Ink asks.

"Some place to put my feet up?" I give him a smile.

He laughs and nods his head. Ink grabs a chair and pillow, placing them in front of me.

"Just relax. The doc is on his way. Should be here any second," Hacker says.

I understand why they want me to get checked out, but at the same time I don't want to be checked out. I just want to sleep or work. I don't want to think about Bear going away to save our daughter, because I'll just worry. Staying awake and not doing anything gives me the opportunity to think about anything and everything.

"I'm here. What's the problem?" Doc walks into the room.

"Jillian had a panic attack. Can you check her over and make sure everything is okay?" Ink asks.

Doc nods his head and walks over to me. He places his bag on the ground and kneels in front of me.

"I'm going to listen to your heartbeat and take your blood pressure," he says.

"Okay," I reply.

Doc takes out his stethoscope and places it on my chest. He tells me to take in deep breaths and moves it around. He then takes out the blood pressure cuff. I try to relax while he does his magic.

"Well, your blood pressure is elevated, but your heartbeat is strong. I want you on bed rest for the rest of today and I'll check you out in the morning," Doc says, taking off the cuff.

I groan and lean my head back. Not bed rest. This is going to kill me even though it's only for one night.

"Ink and Hacker. I want you to watch her. She stays in bed unless she needs to go to the bathroom. You help her to the bathroom and back to bed. I don't want her getting out for anything else." Doc looks over at them.

"Yes, sir," both of them respond.

Great, now I have two people watching me like hawks. Fucking fantastic. Maybe I can find a way to get Ink and Hacker to leave the room and sneak out. I could probably get Antoinette or Cindy to help me escape from them.

"And you, young lady. I know you are going to try to get away from them, but that's not going to happen. Bear told me I'm allowed to do anything within reason to you. If you try to escape, I will handcuff you to the bed," Doc says.

I stare at him with wide eyes. I've never heard doc talk this way and honestly, it makes me want to do what he says.

"Do you understand?" he says. "If I hear anything about you attempting to or thinking about it, I will come back and cuff you to the bed."

I nod my head, not trusting my voice to work.

"I want words. 'I promise not to try to get out of bed, unless I need to use the bathroom,'" he says.

"I promise not to try to get out of bed unless I need to use the bathroom," my voice cracks in the beginning.

I cringe when I hear that, and I can hear Ink and Hacker chuckling at that. I glare at them.

"Don't give Jillian a hard time. If I hear you are, I'll come and put you in your place," he tells the boys.

They straighten up and nod their heads. This time, it's my turn to chuckle at them. I've never seen them be so obedient towards someone. It's a sight to see.

"Now, I'm going to my house but if anything happens, don't hesitate to call," Doc says, packing up his stuff.

"Thanks, doc," I reply.

"And make sure you are drinking plenty of water. Hear that. Water," he says.

I scowl and shake my head. I'm okay drinking water, but it's not my favorite. I would much rather have sweet tea, coffee, hot chocolate, or soda.

"I mean it. It will help you and your baby. I want you to drink over a liter before it hits seven this evening," he tells me.

"Okay, I promise," I reply. "Thanks again."

He nods his head and walks out of the building. I turn towards the guys and watch them talk quietly to themselves.

"Do you think you could call Cindy and ask if she can help me take a shower?" I ask.

"Sorry, Jillian. She's actually away taking care of her mother," Ink says.

Crap. Okay, I can ask Antoinette.

"Antoinette?" I ask.

"I'll call her and see if she is available," Hacker says.

I hope she can. It's not like I need to take a shower, well bath, but I would like one. I took one this morning, but since I worked, I would like to be clean.

Ever since I started working again, I haven't gotten nearly as dirty. Noah and Gears are always there to help lift the heavy things and make sure I'm not doing too much. I sweat so much cause it's hot in the garage, but that's about it.

"Do you want to go upstairs to your room and play some cards while we wait?" Ink asks.

"Sure," I reply.

There's no use just sitting here in an awkward silence. Might as well make our way upstairs so that if Antoinette does come, I'm already up there closer to the bathroom.

"I'll be behind you when you walk up the stairs," Ink says. "Let me grab a water bottle real quick and then we can head upstairs."

I wait for him to grab it. When he comes back, he helps me sit up from the chair.

"I feel like I'm forty pounds heavier than I was with Marcy," I grumble.

I'm huge and I don't know why. We asked the doctor to keep everything a secret, besides the baby's health. It was a decision that Bear and I wanted with everything going on. We wanted something to look forward to if we couldn't get Marcy back.

"Looks like you're carrying twins," Ink says as we walk up the stairs.

"I hope not. I mean, I don't care, but I think one is enough. Maybe this baby is just bigger than Marcy," I reply, out of breath.

I stop at the top of the stairs and take in deep breaths of air.

"Sometimes it does feel like twins," I mutter.

I am almost twice the size I was with Marcy at almost seven months pregnant. I'm worried, but the doc would have said something if he was worried about my size.

I have been eating a lot more than I did with Marcy. I could have easily gained all that weight and it could just be fat.

Ink and I make our way into Bear's and my room. Stepping into the room, I take a deep breath in. This room smells like Bear, and it makes me miss him.

Ink helps me into the bed and places the water bottle right next to me.

"I want you sipping on that," he says.

I nod my head and take a drink. Lemon dances across my taste buds.

"Lemon?" I ask.

"Yep! I know you don't like water by itself. We had some lemons, and I know you like lemons, so I decided to put some in," Ink says, bringing a chair closer to the bed.

"Thanks," I whisper, tears appearing in my eyes.

I sniffle quietly. I don't want Ink to know that I'm starting to cry.

"Please don't cry. I don't do well with women and crying," he says.

I laugh but start crying even more.

"I hate hormones," I chuckle.

"It's going to be okay. How about we take some deep breaths in and out?" he says.

I nod my head and follow his lead. It does help me calm down, but I know anything will make me cry now.

"Hey, Antoinette said she could come in two hours to help you. She has a class she's about to teach," Hacker says, appearing at the doorway.

"Thanks," I mumble.

Hacker nods his head and goes back downstairs. I was really hoping Antoinette would be able to come. I don't really know what to talk about with Ink.

"Have you ever thought about getting a tattoo?" Ink asks.

"I actually have," I reply.

His face turns to shock. "Really?"

"Yeah, I thought about getting a couple of flowers I've drawn. Well, have the tattoo artist probably clean up the lines but use my idea."

He stares at me, his mouth wide open.

"You have to let me tattoo you. Please," he says.

"Okay, that can work. I've also thought about getting Bear's real name tattooed on me. Surprise him," I say, my cheeks turning red.

"Tell me when and where and I'll do it."

"Okay, it'll probably have to be after things settle."

He nods his head. I start to drink again, taking several big gulps of water.

"Do you want to play a card game, rest, or just talk?" Ink asks.

"Talk for a little bit?" I ask.

"We can do that. What do you want to talk about?"

"I don't know. I just need something to keep my mind off of everything. I worry about him. I worry about all of you."

Tears spring in my eyes once again. Maybe this isn't the conversation to have right now.

"Why do you worry?" Ink asks.

"I worry that something is going to happen to you guys. You are my family now and if something happens, I don't know what I'm going to do with myself," I reply.

Ink grabs my hands.

"Nothing is going to happen to us. We are going to be just fine," he says.

I nod my head, trying to believe him.

"It's just a worry. How can I not worry about you guys?" I say.

"I know, Jillian. But we all keep each other safe. We have each other's backs," Ink squeezes my hands.

"Yeah."

They do have each other's backs, but I still worry. They go out and sometimes I don't know if they will come back home. I haven't had a family in a while and when I finally have one; I worry.

I groan when I feel the pressure in my bladder.

"What's wrong?" Ink asks, panic on his face.

"I need to go to the bathroom. Help me?" I ask. "After we can play a card game."

He stands up from his chair and walks towards me. As he

helps me up from the bed, we slowly make our way towards the bathroom.

"I've really got to pee," I whisper.

The next step I take, I feel something run down my legs. I look at Ink with wide eyes.

"Ink," I panic.

He stares at me and then looks down at my legs, his eyes going wide.

CHAPTER TWENTY-ONE

MARCY

"Let's go have some fun with these girls!" someone yells and laughs.

I stir awake but don't open my eyes. I honestly didn't even hear what the person said. All I know is they were yelling.

"Oh, girls! Wake up!" someone yells.

Opening my eyes, I'm met with two men walking towards our cell door. Panic fills me as I see their posture and facial expression. Wicked grins lay on their faces.

I turn to Estella and see her eyes are wide with fear. I'm still so sore from the night before or well early this morning. I've honestly lost track of time and don't even know how long I've been here for.

We have a tiny little window that is barred, letting us see if there is sunlight or not. It looks like the sun is either setting or rising.

"What fun we are going to have with you two. A lot of people are gone, which means it's our turn to be with you," one of them says. "Right Jose?"

"Right, Edwardo," Jose says.

They unlock the door and step into the cell. Panic fills my body as they start to come toward me. I don't have enough strength to fight them off. I'm exhausted and in so much pain.

Estella steps in front of my sitting figure and braces herself.

"Have your fun with me," she says.

I stare at her in horror. You don't invite them to have fun with you. That's one way to get raped by fifteen men and probably not see the next day.

Edwardo grabs Estella's arms and drags her to the other side of the room.

"No, please don't hurt her!" I yell.

Jose looks at me and grins. He steps toward me and yanks me up on my feet.

"Take me! Please! Just please! Not her!" Estella screams.

I watch as Edwardo punches her, making her scream in pain.

"I think Jose is going to have fun with his girl. Don't you think, Jose?" Edwardo says.

Jose licks his lips, eyeing my body. "Fuck yeah. I can't wait to pound into your tight cunt. If you're a good girl, I'll even let you finish."

I try to cover my body, not wanting his eyes on me any longer. I never got a pair of clothes from the last time the three men raped me. They left, and I had to let their semen dry on me. I still have it in my hair and on my body now.

"Looks like she's already been marked. I'll have to add on to it. Cover you in my semen. Letting you know that you are dirt. A whore and nothing more. You'll always be a whore," he says.

I pull against his arm, trying to get out of his hold.

"Did you like being marked?" he asks. "I think you do, since you let it dry on you."

He yanks my body forward, making me tumble into his body.

"Always a whore," he whispers in my ear.

He forces me onto my knees. Holding my hair in his hand, he takes his other one and unbuckles his pants.

"Take my cock in your mouth like a good little slut," he says, pulling his dick out of his pants.

Right as he's about to stick his cock in my mouth, his body moves away from me. I watch with wide eyes as Noah stabs a knife into his chest and twists it. Noah pulls the knife out and stabs it back into the guy, making him make gurgling noises.

I start to feel bile rise in my throat. I take in a long, shaky breath, trying to calm myself down. I move into the corner and watch as everything happens.

Butch kills the other guy and before I know it, both of them are dead. I look back at Noah and watch as he takes in the whole room, his face turning mad.

What is he doing here? How did they get here? I'm relieved, but I'm also in shock at everything that just happened. Noah just killed a guy, and he doesn't seem fazed by it. Why isn't he fazed by it? He told me that he's never killed anyone before. Shouldn't he be in shock that he just murdered someone?

"Please, no," someone mumbles.

My head swings towards the left, and I watch as Butch tries to talk to Estella. I want to move and help her, tell her that she doesn't have to be afraid. That Butch is a good guy, but my body won't move. My body is frozen.

I hug my legs closer to my body, trying to cover myself up. Footsteps fill the room, and more faces appear. My dad, Gears, Phantom, and Whiskey. I feel my body start to shake. Too many faces.

I know subconsciously that I don't need to be afraid of them. I know them, but my mind sees males, which immediately puts me in panic mode. They can hurt us. Do so many wicked things to us and not feel bad at all.

My body starts to shake, and I move my eyes to the ground. Don't look at them in the eyes. Don't do anything and maybe they won't see me. Maybe I will just blend into the wall, and they'll leave.

"Marcy?" Noah whispers.

My eyes snap up, looking him straight in the eyes. He won't want me once he finds out what they did to me. He'll throw me to the curb and never look back. Everyone will hate me once they find out. I don't even think my own parents will want me after they find out. No one will. I'll be alone forever.

He takes a step toward me, and I huddle closer to the wall. I don't want him close to me. Keep him at arm's length and he'll move on. He doesn't need to know what happened. He can just leave me here.

"It's okay, Marcy. We're going to take you home and get you all cleaned up," he whispers.

I watch as he broadens his shoulders and takes another step closer to me. I let out a little whimper and bury my head in my knees, but make sure that I can keep an eye on him in case he tries to do something.

"Marcy," he says.

I don't acknowledge him. Maybe he'll leave me alone if I ignore him.

"Marcy, look at me," he says.

He knows I'm looking at him, through the corner of my eyes, but that isn't enough for him. Is he going to make me look into his eyes and then humiliate me like everyone else has?

"Please, look at me," desperation fills his voice.

I fully look at him, just embracing that I may get humiliated later on. What surprises me is that he's on his knees with tears in his eyes. I've never seen him with tears in his eyes. I haven't seen someone look at me like he is right now, in a long time.

"Can you stand up?" he asks.

I shake my head. I don't want to stand up. I don't want my body on display. I don't want to give him easy access to my body. So many thoughts run through my mind that I don't realize he's taken off his shirt and is handing it to me.

I flinch when his arm comes closer to me. He gives me a sad smile but continues to hold his hand out. I quickly take his shirt and pull it on, worried he's going to rip it out of my hands and laugh at me.

"Can you stand up now?" he asks.

I don't move. I see another figure walk up and realize that it's my dad.

"Marcy?" his voice is hoarse like he's trying to keep so many emotions down.

I stare at him but don't feel anything.

"Can you stand up for us?" he whispers.

I give up and stand. They both take timid steps toward me, wrapping their arms around me. My body is stiff, and I don't hug back. I don't feel anything. I feel numb. So much has gone on that I just want to sleep and never wake up.

"Please, no," Estella cries out.

My eyes go wide when I recognize the panic in her voice. I push against my dad and Noah, catching them off guard. Their arms unwrap from me, and I dash towards Estella. Butch is trying to put a shirt on her, but she is panicking. I quickly grab her hand and pull her towards the corner of the room. Wrapping my arms around her, I force ourselves to sit on the ground; me covering Estella's body with mine. Pure instincts come over me, and I make sure that she is safe, my back completely exposed to their attacks.

I hear cussing coming from the guys, but I don't pay attention. I just need to keep Estella safe.

"Marcy?" someone whispers.

I don't look back. I don't want to see their facial expressions.

What if they're mad at me for hiding Estella? What if they decide they are going to beat me instead?

"We aren't going to hurt you," Noah says.

I look over my shoulder and take in everyone's faces. Most of them have sad facial expressions. My dad though, his face is a mixture of disbelief, sadness, and anger all in one. I don't think I've seen that many emotions from him.

"It's okay," Noah says. "Everything is going to be okay."

A loud noise goes off in the room, making Estella and I scream. I watch as my dad takes out his phone and answers it.

Estella is trembling in my arms as my dad yells into the phone. I'm not paying attention to what he's saying, but I can tell he's panicking and worried.

My dad turns around and stares at us.

"Something is wrong with Jillian. She's being taken to the hospital. We need to leave now and head back home," he says.

What's wrong with mom?

"Come on, Marcy. We can talk in the van," Noah says.

Everyone is panicking about my mom going to the hospital. It's like they know something is going on with my mom.

"They're going to take us back to the compound," I whisper to Estella.

She looks into my eyes, fear evident in them. I know how she feels. Even though I know these people, I'm still scared out of my mind. They could have changed while I was gone. Realized that they didn't need me but now just want to torture me.

Estella nods her head and I help us stand up. Our legs are shaky, and I feel like I'm going to collapse at any moment.

"We have a doctor waiting in the van that will look over you," Noah says.

I nod my head and watch all of them carefully. Whiskey, my dad, and Phantom walk in front of us. Noah, Butch, and Gears walk behind us.

Estella and I stiffen when they walk behind us. I don't like not being able to see what they are doing. They could be planning this and attack us from behind. Knock us over and have their way with us. Beat us until we are on the brink of death.

"Relax, we aren't going to hurt you," Butch says.

My body stiffens even more. I've heard that before. Some men, in the beginning, would say they aren't going to hurt us, and then they would. They are the worse. They got off on our shocked and scared faces when we realized that it was all a lie, and they were going to have their way with us or beat us.

Someone curses behind us and I feel Estella's body start to shake. I bring her closer to my body as we walk up the stairs. I don't like this one bit. Everything in my mind is going off, saying we are in danger.

"Follow us. Our van is through the forest," Noah whispers.

We continue walking towards the forest. The hair on my arms starts sticking up and chills run down my body. I have a bad feeling about walking into the forest.

I stop walking and make Estella stop. Heat radiates from the body behind us.

"Why'd you stop walking?" Butch asks.

I stare at the forest and shake my head. No way in hell am I walking into the forest. There could be something on the other side. Something bad could happen to us.

"There are some men in the forest that are with us. We wanted back up, in case something went wrong. They won't hurt you," Noah says.

I still don't trust them. They could be saying that to get us to go through, and once we make it into the forest, they pounce on us. I shake my head again.

"If anything happens to you, I'll deal with them," my dad says.

I stare into his eyes and see that he is being honest. I take in a deep breath and nod my head. I want to get off of this compound. I don't fully trust my dad and what he says, but if it means getting off this compound, I'll trust him.

My dad sighs in relief and gives me a smile.

"Okay, let's get going. I don't want to be away from Jillian for long," he says.

He starts walking again, and I have to force myself to take a step forward.

"Just through these trees and we'll be at the van," Noah says.

I look at my feet as we walk through part of the forest, not wanting to trip on any roots. After a while, we make it to a clearing where two vans are.

"Let's get you to the doctor and on the road," Butch says.

The only thing running through my head as we make our way toward the van is I don't want to be separated from Estella. I will fight to stay with her.

"Doc, can you make a quick assessment of the girls? We need to get on the road," my dad asks.

"Why don't you stay the night? It's a seven-hour drive and you must be exhausted," someone says.

I don't recognize this person. My breathing starts to pick up. Are they giving us to them?

"I can't. Jillian is being rushed to the hospital right now and I need to get back there," my dad replies.

The person nods, and another guy walks towards us. Estella and I take a step back, running into someone. I look up and realize it's Butch.

"It's just the doc. You don't have to be afraid. Let him look you over, real quick," he says.

I look back toward the doc and realize he is right in front of us. Estella and I stand still as he quickly looks over our bodies. I honestly don't know what he did, but he doesn't seem happy.

"When you get back to the compound, have them checked over again. They are severely underweight from the looks of it. They might be hiding things underneath the clothes, but they should be able to travel for seven hours," the guy says.

"Thanks," my dad says.

The doctor walks back towards the van.

"Let's get you in the other van and we can head home," Butch says

He gently places his hands on our backs and pushes us forward. We both stiffen, not used to men touching us with gentleness. The back of the van opens, and they help us in.

"We'll be in front and behind you on our bikes. If you need to stop, just let Whiskey know and he'll stop for you," Noah says.

I nod my head but know that I'm not going to say anything to Whiskey. Noah gives me a smile before closing the door.

I bring Estella closer to my body and rest my head against the van. Maybe I can catch up on some sleep. Estella snuggles into my side, and I let out a content sigh.

The van starts moving and soft music starts playing, lulling me to sleep.

CHAPTER TWENTY-TWO

JILLIAN

His eyes are wide, and they make me panic more. Did I pee my pants? I feel my cheeks heat up, but I look down to see.

Red.

A little red stream is running down my leg.

A little red stream.

Red.

Oh my goodness, it's blood.

Panic sets in. I look back up at Ink and see that he is staring at my legs.

"Ink," I whisper.

Oh my goodness. This can't be happening. My baby.

"Hospital," I say.

He continues to stare down at my legs, panic all over his face.

"Ink!" I yell, snapping him out of his thoughts.

He stares into my eyes, so many emotions running through them.

"Hospital," I repeat.

He nods his head and picks me up bridal style. Ink doesn't

look big, but oh, is he strong. He fast walks out of my room and down the stairs.

"Hacker! Get the car ready!" he yells, making his way into the living room.

Hacker looks up from his phone and takes the scene in. His eyes go wide before he jumps up off the couch and grabs the keys. He runs towards the door, leaving it open.

Ink carries me out of the house and places me into the car, sliding in right next to me.

What is happening to me? Am I having a miscarriage? Tears appear in my eyes when I think of that. I don't want to have a miscarriage.

"I want Bear," I whisper.

I just want to be in his arms. I just want him to reassure me. Be with me and tell me everything is going to be alright even if things aren't.

"Drive faster!" Ink yells at Hacker.

Hacker starts cursing and picks up the speed.

"Try to calm down for me, Jillian," Ink says to me. "Deep breaths in."

I try to take a deep breath in, but it turns into a sob, and I can't help it.

"I just want Bear," I tell Ink.

"I'll call Bear right now. You just need to take a couple of deep breaths in," he says.

I close my eyes and try to calm down. I can hear Ink on the phone.

"Bear, you need to head home now! We're taking Jillian to the hospital," Ink says.

I don't know how long he's on the phone for. It doesn't seem like a long time, but I hear him mutter a couple of words.

"Hacker. When we get to the hospital, I'm going to need

you to run in and get a bed for us. I'll help Jillian out of the car," Ink says.

"Got it," Hacker replies.

The car comes to a halt, and I hear car doors opening and closing. Opening my eyes, Ink helps me out of the car.

"Bear," I whisper.

"He's on his way," Ink replies.

He picks me up and makes his way toward the hospital. Nurses and doctors meet us at the entrance with a bed.

"Place her on here," a lady says.

Ink places me on the bed, letting go of my hand. I start to panic. I don't want to be alone.

"Ink!" I call out.

"I'm right here," he says.

I hold out my hand, wanting him to grab it.

"Sir, you can't come back with us," the same lady says.

"Please," I cry. "Ink, don't leave me."

"I'm coming with you," Ink says

"Sir, you really can't come with us," the nurse says.

"Please, Ink. I'm scared," I whisper.

"Lady, I'm coming whether you like it or not. Jillian is scared, and I'm not about to leave her while her husband is in a different state," Ink growls at her.

The nurse goes quiet, and I feel Ink grab my hand. I squeeze it and he squeezes right back. A little weight is lifted off my shoulders, but I'm still worried about what's wrong with me.

"Keep up," the nurse tells Ink.

"Place her in one of the examination rooms. We'll look at her and see what's wrong," the doctor says.

"What happened?" A nurse asks Ink.

Tears are still streaming down my face as Ink starts to talk.

"Our doctor put her on bed rest. She's been under a lot of

stress for the past two months. We went to go to the bathroom and blood started to run down her legs," Ink says.

The situation starts to sink in more as he talks about it. Blood was running down my leg. Oh my goodness. Blood was running down my leg.

"We'll take a look and see if there is anything wrong," the nurse says.

The bed stops moving and I feel people grabbing my legs and propping them up. My dress slides up and I feel someone pulling my underwear down.

Nurses hook machines up to me, and I can hear a steady heartbeat. My heartbeat.

"I'm scared," I say, turning my face towards Ink's.

"Everything is going to be okay. I'm right here. Bear is on his way," Ink whispers.

I feel some poking and prodding making me wince. My heart rate starts to pick up, making the machine beep out of control.

"Ma'am, I'm going to need you to calm down. Everything is going to be alright," a young nurse says.

"Take deep breaths in for me." Ink squeezes my hand.

I follow his breathing and slowly calm myself down. I feel my legs being placed back down on the bed.

"Alright, well, good and bad news," the doctor says.

My heart sinks.

"Bad news then good," I say.

I don't want to hear any bad news, but I know I can't be oblivious to this. I need to know what happened or what could happen.

"Bad news is, if you continue to stress and work your body up, we are going to have to do an emergency C-section." The doctor walks right next to me. "The good news is you didn't have a miscarriage."

Tears appear in my eyes. I don't want to have a C-section. I still have two months left until my baby is due.

"I am only seven months pregnant," I reply. "What's going to happen if you do the C-section? Is my baby going to be okay?"

The doctor's face turns into shock. "Seven months?"

"Yes, I'm seven months. Now, is my baby going to be okay if you do a C-section?" I ask.

I can feel myself start to panic. I don't want anything to happen to the baby. I don't want to have a C-section.

"Your baby should be okay. He or she will be a preemie, but we will do our best to make sure the baby lives," he says.

I let out a little sigh of relief. I would hate for anything to happen to the baby.

"Now, can you stay calm on your own or do you want us to give you something?" the doctor asks.

"I don't want to be knocked out," I reply. "I don't care. I just don't want to be knocked out."

"Alright, nurse can you give her something to calm her down but not knock her out?" the doctor asks, turning to the nurse.

The nurse nods and leaves the room. I feel anxious. I don't like being in hospitals. They make me itchy and antsy.

"I know you hate hospitals, but just try to be calm," Ink says.

I nod my head and relax against the pillows. All of the sudden, I am very aware of my full bladder.

"I need to pee," I say.

"I would rather you not get out of bed, but if he can carry you to the bathroom, then you may use it. If he can't, then I am going to get a bedpan or we can put a catheter in," the doctor replies.

"He can carry me," I reply, not giving Ink enough time to respond.

"Great. I have rounds to do, but the nurse will be back in

here at any moment with the medicine," the doctor says, walking out of the room.

I turn towards Ink and give him a sheepish smile.

"Sorry, I don't fancy using a bedpan," I reply.

He laughs and shakes his head. "That's alright. Now, you're going to hold on to your pole while I carry you into the bathroom."

I nod my head and grab onto it. He gently places his hands under my knees and around my back, picking me up. Ink walks to the bathroom and places my feet on the ground.

"You go to the bathroom and when you are done, call me in. I'll take you back to bed," he says. "Do you understand me? I don't want you to walk at all or else I'm going to get them to put a catheter in you and tie you to the bed."

My face pales and I nod my head. I definitely don't want that to happen to me. That would kill me if that happened.

Ink leaves the bathroom while I do my business. I let out an audible sigh when the pressure is relieved off my bladder. Standing up, I pull my underwear up.

"Ink?" I call out.

He opens the door, walks in, picks me up, and makes his way back into the room. Gently placing me down on the bed, he helps me get situated before sitting down in the chair beside me.

"Hello, I'm Michelle and I will be your nurse for the next six hours before a new nurse comes in," Michelle says.

"How long am I here for? The doctor didn't say," I reply.

"He wants to keep you overnight. Just in case something happens and to watch your vital signs."

My head hits the pillows as I let out a groan. Great, now I'm going to have several other eyes on me to make sure I follow the rules.

"Now, I'm going to hook this up to you in your IV and it will help keep you calm. May make you a little drowsy," she says.

I nod my head and let her do her job. I turn to Ink and look him in the eyes.

"I don't like this one bit," I reply.

He laughs. "I know, but it's going to be okay. We can talk or you can take a nap and if anything changes with Bear or here, I'll wake you up."

"I don't want to sleep."

The nurse chuckles before she leaves the room, saying she'll be back later to check in on me.

"I know, but it may help you. You may feel better, or it can help pass the time. Bear has another six hours before he's here," Ink says.

Six hours is a long time. I know it'll feel like eternity if I stay awake.

"I'll take a little nap, I guess. Is that okay?" I ask.

"Yes, I'll be right here the whole time. I won't leave you," he says.

I nod my head and lay back down, getting comfortable. The medicine is slowly working on me as I feel my eyes droop close.

* * *

I GROAN as a dull pain spreads across my stomach.

"Jillian?" Ink whispers.

I hum, not wanting to wake up yet.

"What's wrong?" he asks.

"Pain," I reply.

Pain. It finally registers in my head. Pain in my stomach.

My eyes fly open, and I look down at my lap. Nothing looks wrong, but I'm in pain.

"I'll call a nurse," Ink says.

He jumps up from his chair and runs towards the door.

"I need a nurse! Jillian is in pain!" he yells.

I watch as he stays close to the door, looking back at me every once in a while. Ink steps back into the room as two nurses walk into the room.

"My stomach, it hurts so bad," I groan in pain.

Panic crosses their faces, and one of them runs out of the room. The other nurse walks closer to me.

"Where exactly is it hurting?" she asks.

"My lower stomach," I reply.

Before she could say anything, the doctor and nurse run into the room.

"Lower abdomen pain," the nurse next to me says.

"Prep for surgery. We're going to have to do an emergency C-section," the doc says.

The two nurses take hold of my bed and start wheeling me out of the room.

"Ink," I cry out.

I don't want to be alone. I don't think I can do this alone.

"I'm right here," he says.

"Sir, since you aren't her husband or family, I'm going to have to ask you to stay in the waiting room," one of the nurses says.

I start to panic. My breathing picks up.

"No, I don't want to be alone," I cry.

The nurses completely ignore me as they continue to wheel my bed towards the operating room.

"Wait!" someone yells.

My heart stops beating. I know that voice. The nurses continue their job with me in the bed.

"I'm her husband!" the person yells.

They stop the bed, and I look around, realizing that we are in the operating room. I hope they allow Bear into the room. I want him here with me as I go through this.

Bear stands right next to me, holding my hand as they start to prep me.

"I'm so scared," I whisper.

"I know, but I'm right here. Everything is going to be okay," he whispers.

CHAPTER TWENTY-THREE

JILLIAN

Bear leans down and kisses my forehead. Tears spring to my eyes and Bear grabs my hands. I'm so scared something is going to go wrong. What if the baby dies? The baby is going to be two months early.

"I'm right here. You are doing amazing," he says.

He wipes away my tears and gives me a smile. I let out a little sigh, knowing Bear will be with me every step of the way. I don't have to worry as much because he is going to take care of me. Make sure that I'm okay.

"I love you," he whispers.

"I love you too," I reply, taking in a deep breath.

A nurse walks up right next to us, giving us a smile.

"We're going to place this curtain over your chest while we do the C-section. We are also going to be numbing your lower half, so you won't feel anything," a nurse says.

"Okay," I whisper.

Right as I say that I feel a little prick in my back. A little cry escapes my mouth.

"You're okay," he whispers in my ear.

I try to relax my mind. I have no doubt my panicking over everything is going to make this C-section worse.

"Take my mind off of this. How was your drive?" I ask.

A seven-hour drive, and I bet he only stopped to get gas and nothing else. Normally they'll stretch their legs, but I bet he didn't even do that. He probably just wanted to get here.

"Marcy," I whisper before he can speak. "Oh my goodness. How is she? You did get her, right?"

"Shhh, calm down. Let's take a couple of deep breaths before I say anything," he whispers, running his hands through my hair.

"Sir, I'm going to need you to put these on," a nurse says.

I watch as his head turns, and he nods. He lets go of one of my hands.

"I'm going to put this on really quick while you take a couple of deep breaths. You won't even know I'm gone," Bear says.

He steps away while I take in slow, deep breaths and let them out. I feel myself starting to calm down some, but I still feel anxious without Bear right next to me.

"Leo?" I ask. "I'm right here," Bear responds.

He grabs my hands and sits down on the chair. He starts to run his hand through my hair, calming me even more down.

"That's it. You're doing an amazing job," he whispers.

I give him a small smile.

"Now, we have Marcy. She is in the hospital, waiting for you to be done. We also rescued another girl," Bear says.

"That's good. I'm glad they are both okay," I reply.

Bear chuckles. "I knew you wouldn't even bat an eyelash that another girl came. That you would just accept her."

"I don't want to worry you, but Marcy is a little different. It's probably the shock from being rescued," Bear says.

Before I can respond, I watch as Bear looks across the curtain and his face pales.

"What's wrong?" I ask, starting to feel myself panic.

He doesn't respond, but his eyes continue to stare at whatever he's looking at.

"Don't pass out on us, sir," one of the nurses says

That brings Bear out of his thoughts. He shakes his head and looks at me, his face still pale.

"What happened?" I ask.

"He was just watching us take out the baby. Nothing to worry about," the nurse says.

I continue to stare at Bear. He's taking deep breaths in and slowly regains the color back on his face. All of the sudden, we hear a cry from the baby.

"It's a boy," the nurse says.

She walks around and shows us a small little baby boy and my heart melts. I'm so in love with him already, and I haven't even seen him for a full minute yet.

"Michael Rodriguez," I whisper.

"I love it," Bear whispers.

The nurse smiles and walks away with Michael. All of the sudden, we hear another cry. I look at Bear with a shocked but curious face.

"Congratulations, you have another baby boy," another nurse says.

I'm stunned. I didn't think I would be pregnant with twins. I guess that explains why I was so big for seven months.

The nurse shows us the baby boy and my heart melts even more. Tears appear in my eyes and I can't help but let out a little cry. I carried these baby boys for seven months.

"Oliver Rodriguez," Bear says.

I nod my head. "I agree."

Even though it was unexpected, I know it's going to be

amazing. Bear is a great dad and I know some of the other guys in the MC will step up and be great uncles. These boys are about to be spoiled.

The nurse walks away with Oliver.

"We're going to stitch you up now. Once we're done, you'll be wheeled back into the room you were in before and can have guests. I do suggest you getting some rest, but I know you have people waiting for you," the doctor says.

I start to feel a tugging on my stomach, but no pain. It makes me feel sick to my stomach, but I try to get my mind off of it.

"Are you okay?" I ask.

"You're asking me if I'm okay and you're the one that's cut open?" he asks.

I stare at him, waiting for him to respond to me.

"A little sick, but I'm okay," he sighs.

He starts running his hand through my hair as he watches my face.

"I'm so proud of you," he whispers.

Tears spring to my eyes. That means so much to me right now.

"Shh. Please don't cry. I didn't mean to make you cry," he says.

"Thank you," I reply.

He gives me a smile. We continue to look into each other's eyes, oblivious to what's happening around us.

"Twin boys," he whispers in disbelief.

"They are going to be a handful. I can just feel it," I say, chuckling at the end.

He laughs and nods his head. "Everyone is going to spoil them rotten. They spoiled Marcy."

"Don't remind me of that. It got so bad I had to start threatening some of the guys."

He stares at me in disbelief. "No, you did not. Really?"

I nod my head. I guess he never found out about that. I didn't try to keep it a secret, but I didn't want Marcy to be a spoiled brat when she got older.

"Alright, Ms. Rodriguez. We are all done here. The nurse will wheel you back into your room and explain things to you," the doc says.

"Thanks," Bear and I say together.

The curtain is removed, and I look down at my stomach. I didn't think it would be exposed, but I also kind of wanted to see how they stitched me up.

"Alright, Mr. Rodriguez, you can follow us," the nurse says.

They start to wheel me out of the room.

"Now, we are doing some tests on your boys to see if they need to stay in the NICU or not. You should find out if they need to in a couple of hours. In the meantime, you'll be numb for some time. You can have visitors, but only during the visiting hours," she explains.

"What about my husband? Can he stay after hours?" I ask.

"Not technically, but we normally bend the rules for the husband here if the patient is healthy enough and they don't get in the way."

I glance at Bear.

"Don't get in the way, please," I whisper

"I won't," he replies.

The nurse wheels me into my room.

"Do you need anything from me?" she asks.

"How long will I be here for?" I ask.

"It can be a day or more. We want to keep you for observation in case anything happens."

I nod my head.

"Thank you," I reply.

"Welcome. If you need me or any nurse, just press this button." She points to the red button right next to my bed.

"Thank you," Bear says.

She nods her head and walks towards the door but stops.

"Visitors. Do you want them?" she asks.

"Yes, please," I reply.

She leaves the room.

"I'm exhausted," I tell Bear.

"I know, baby. We can visit with the guys and Marcy, and then you can rest all you want," he replies.

Before I can say anything, Butch, Ink, Gears, and Noah walk into the room. I look at their feet and can see two smaller pairs, Marcy and the other girl.

"How are you feeling, Jillian?" Gears asks.

"Tired, but okay," I reply.

Marcy and the other girl continue to stand behind the guys. I just want to see Marcy and see if she is okay.

"Marcy?" I say.

I watch as the guys step more into the room and part ways for Marcy and the other girl. I choke back a sob when I take in their appearance. They are both skinny and have bruises on their faces and arms. I bet they have more bruises on their body, but it's covered by their clothes.

"Come here, baby," I say, holding my arms out.

She hesitantly takes a step forward with the girl. It breaks my heart to see them like this. I don't even know the other girl, but I can tell she's been through a lot.

Marcy takes another hesitant step closer to me and steps into my embrace.

"Oh, it's so good to have you back," I whisper into her ear. "I love you."

Marcy just hugs me back before letting go. She immediately goes back to the other girl and wraps her arms around her.

"What's your name?" I ask.

"Estella," she whispers.

Such a pretty name. Estella and Marcy go sit down in the chairs. I look around the room and realize Noah and Butch are both watching them carefully. They both have the same look in their eyes and I wonder if Butch has found his girl.

There is a big age gap, but Butch is so sweet. Any girl would be lucky to have him as a partner.

"Knock. Knock," a nurse says, walking into the room.

I stare at her as she wheels in two smaller beds.

"I just wanted to bring in the twins so everyone can see them. They do need to stay at the hospital for a couple of days to monitor them," she says.

All the boys stare at me in shock.

"Twins?" Gears chokes out.

"Surprise!" I say, chuckling at the end.

"Oh my goodness. They are so adorable," Butch whispers.

Everyone else walks closer to the two small cots holding the babies. The males coo at them and exclaim how cute they are.

"Michael and Oliver Rodriguez," Bear tells them.

"They are going to be spoiled rotten when they get out of the hospital. No one is going to be able to leave them alone," Butch says.

"I agree. Everyone is going to want to hold them and spoil them," Gears says.

"I'll have to keep you guys from spoiling them too much," I say, chuckling.

Both of them snort and shake their heads.

"Jillian says they're going to be troublemakers," Bear says.

"Oh yeah, if they hang around us, they will be," Gears laughs.

I look over at Marcy and Estella. They are both staring at Oliver and Michael with an expression I can't read. I don't know what they are thinking, and I wish I did.

As if she could feel me staring at her, Marcy looks up and

over at me and I give her a small smile. She doesn't give me one back I stare into her eyes and realize they look a little glossed over.

"I'm tired. Noah, can you take us back to the compound?" Marcy whispers.

My face falls. Does she not want to be here right now?

Noah nods his head. "Yeah, I can. I'll drive the van. I'll tell Whiskey that I'm taking the van and he'll take my bike."

"Stay safe. Text me when you get the girls back to the compound," Bear says.

"I'll go with them," Butch says. "Follow on my bike."

Marcy looks at us and gives us a fake smile. It breaks my heart even more and I try to hold my tears back. Once they get out of the room, I burst into tears.

"Shh. It's going to be okay. She's been through a lot. We need to give her some time to settle into this life again. She'll be okay," Bear whispers.

"Give them a couple of days to get used to being back here. Don't pressure them into talking but try to be engaging with them," Gears says.

Bear wraps his arms around my shoulders and hugs me. The nurse clears her throat, making us aware that she is still in the room. I had completely forgotten that she was here.

"I'm going to take the twins back. You get some rest," she says.

Before any of us can say anything, she is walking out of the room with the boys.

"We'll leave you guys," Gears says.

"You can stay if you want. I may just fall asleep, but don't leave because of me," I whisper, exhaustion taking a toll on my body.

They all nod and sit down in their chairs. They softly talk to each other as I fall asleep.

CHAPTER TWENTY-FOUR

MARCY

We made it to the house several minutes ago. Estella and I are currently sitting in the living room, Butch and Noah are sitting across from us.

We aren't talking to each other. Butch and Noah are quietly talking to each other, looking at us every once in a while. They've tried to get us to talk with them, but Estella and I both stay quiet.

The quiet has left me to my thoughts, and I don't know if that's a good thing. I left the hospital because I didn't know how to act around them. I didn't know if they expected certain things out of me. It was killing me not knowing because I didn't want to do something wrong.

The longer we sit here in silence the more I think about how I don't fit in here anymore. Everything has changed. People don't look at me the same and my mom was pregnant. How did I not know that my mom was pregnant? She wasn't showing when I got taken.

I'm hurt that my dad or any of the guys didn't say anything during the seven-hour drive. I was left in my worry about my mom not knowing why she was going to the hospital. Then I find out that I have twin brothers now.

It's like they knew something was going to happen and decided to get pregnant. Replace me with two baby boys if they decided not to get me back. My heart breaks thinking about that. Maybe I was better off staying with my kidnappers.

At least I knew how I was supposed to act. Even though I got beaten and raped daily, I knew what was expected of me. Maybe Dom would have kept me safer, but thinking back on it, he couldn't have given away that he knew me.

Dom. Did he make it out okay?

"What happened to Dom?" I say my voice cracking at the end.

Butch and Noah's heads whip in our direction, their eyes wide open.

"He made it out and is at the doctor's getting checked over," Noah says.

I nod my head. I care, but at the same time I don't know him, so I don't care. I don't know how to feel and it's making me frustrated.

I feel angry, annoyed, scared, frustrated, and so many more emotions that I just feel numb. I don't know how to feel and so my brain is making me feel numb.

The boys continue to look at us, and I don't know what to do. Are they expecting me to continue on the conversation? I don't know what to say to them.

Anxiety fills my stomach as they continue to stare at us. I look over at Estella and realize she's looking at her lap. No doubt she can feel their stares on us.

A tingly sensation fills my chest, and I start to scratch it. The longer they stare at me, the more intense the tingle sensation gets. It feels like I can't breathe.

"I'm going to get water," I say, my voice higher than normal.

Right as I stand up, Estella's hand grabs my wrist making me freeze. I look down at her and watch as her body starts to shake.

"I'll be back," I whisper.

She lets go of my hand, but never once does she look up from her lap. I feel her pain, probably not to the full extent. I know these people, yet at the same time it feels like I don't know them. I haven't looked any of them in the eyes.

You always look at the chest unless they request you to look in their eyes. They generally never want you to look them in the eyes.

I wonder if they don't want you to look in their eyes because they will feel guilty. Would they feel guilty? I highly doubt it. They are evil people. I don't even know if they can feel emotions.

I make my way into the kitchen and lean up against the counter. I'm going to give it a couple of days, but I may just take Estella and leave. Try to start fresh somewhere else.

I don't know how to act around anyone here. It's like I'm walking on eggshells afraid that if I step or say something wrong, they will blow up on me.

Taking in a shaky breath, I stand up straight and grab a glass. My hands are shaky as I fill the glass full of tap water. I take a big gulp of the water and place the cup down.

What am I going to do? I want to ask what they expect of me, but at the same time they may not like that. That may be one of the rules; don't speak unless given permission. Which I've already spoken out of turn, so maybe that's not it. Maybe they don't want you asking too many questions.

I can feel myself starting to overthink and give myself a headache, but I can't stop. Even though I spent my whole life living here, it feels so foreign. It's like I'm stepping into this compound for the first time, and I don't know how to act.

"Are you okay?" Noah asks.

I jump, knocking over my glass into the sink. My heart is hammering against my chest as I take shallow breaths of air. Where did he come from? I slowly turn around and see Noah standing in the doorway with his hands up.

"Sorry, I didn't mean to scare you," he says. "You've just been in here a while, and I wanted to make sure that you are okay."

I stare at him, not knowing what to do. Do I answer his question or just leave it be? I don't even know if he really was asking for me to answer.

"I'm glad we got you back. Nothing has been the same around here," Noah says, taking a step into the kitchen.

My body stiffens as he takes a step closer, and I keep my eyes on his chest. I don't like that he is taking steps closer to me. I don't know what he's going to do.

He's changed while I was gone. I watched him kill that person with my own eyes and I don't know how to feel about that. Noah has never been a killer, and it makes me sick thinking that he killed someone. But at the same time, I find it attractive that he would kill someone for me. To get me back.

"What's going on inside your head?" he asks.

I shake my head. So much is going on in my head that I don't even know how to put them into words. I wouldn't even know where to start.

"Marcy?" he whispers.

I keep my eyes on his chest. Out of my peripherals, I can see him giving me a worried look and I don't know how I feel about that. Is he faking it to get me to open up and then will pounce on me once I do? That's what worries me. I can't read them. I don't know what to expect and it's stressing me out.

"Hey, it's okay. No one is going to hurt you here," he says, taking a step closer to me.

Out of instinct, I take a step back. My body is buzzing with adrenaline, anticipating what he's going to do. I look around the kitchen to find my escape routes. There's only one, and Noah is in my way.

What am I going to do if this goes south? What can I use to defend myself if he comes at me?

I look around again and see a pan sitting on the counter. I pick it up and groan with how heavy it is. I don't know how long I'll be able to hold this up. Would I even be able to swing this hard enough to hurt him and be able to get away?

I look back at Noah's chest and see his face contort into shock. His hands go up again and he takes a step back.

"Marcy, you can put that down. I'm not going to hurt you," he says.

I don't believe him. How can a male not hurt a female? All men have this desire in them to hurt people. I just know it. Maybe Noah was hiding it before I got taken, but I can see it now. The way his eyes turned cold and animalistic when he killed that person.

"You're going to hurt yourself. I promise I won't hurt you." He takes another step back.

My arms start to shake in protest. I didn't think a pan could be so heavy. I drop the pan onto the counter and take a deep breath in. My muscles ache and all I want to do is sit down and rest.

"Marcy, can you look me in the eyes?" Noah asks.

I continue to stare at his chest, not feeling comfortable at all. I know he asked me to, and essentially gave me permission, but at the same time it doesn't feel right.

"Come on. You won't get in trouble. Look me in the eyes," he says.

I slowly move my eyes up and make eye contact with him. He gives me a smile.

"Good girl." His smile widens.

Something flips in my stomach when he calls me a good girl and I don't know what it is, but I like it. I let out a small sigh.

"You're such a good girl. Nothing's going to happen to you," he says.

There he goes again, calling me a good girl. I can feel my body start to relax, which scares me. My body immediately stiffens. What is going on with me? I have to be on alert around these people.

"It's okay to relax. Nothing's going to happen to you," Noah softly speaks. "I'll keep you safe here."

Before my mind can wonder, I hear an hear a piercing scream. Estella. What is Butch doing to her? My eyes go wide as I look at the only exit, right where Noah is standing.

I so badly want to go to Estella and see what's wrong, but he's standing in my way. How am I going to get past him? As if he can hear my thoughts, he moves to the side.

I quickly sprint out of the kitchen and into the living room. I take in the whole room. Butch has a panicked face on as he stares at Estella. He's standing right next to his chair and Estella is curled up in a ball on the couch.

Making my way towards her, I don't even think about Butch being in the way. My only concern is on Estella and making sure she is okay.

I wrap my arms around Estella the best I can.

"It's okay. You're safe," I whisper into her ear.

I can feel her body shaking in my arms and I know the guys being in the same room isn't helping her calm down. I look up and find Noah's chest. Taking in a deep breath, I try to muster up as much courage as I can.

"Are we allowed to go to my room?" I whisper.

"Oh course. You don't need to ask for permission," he replies.

I nod my head and help Estella up from the couch. The whole time her head is looking down. I hold her body close to mine as we make our way up the stairs and into my room. Helping Estella sit on my bed, I hold her the best I can against my body.

"Everything is okay. I'm right here and I'll keep you safe," I speak softly to her.

Slowly, her body starts to stop shaking, but she's still clinging onto me.

"You want to tell me what happened?" I ask.

She slowly lifts her head up and looks at me.

"He tried making conversation with me, but I didn't respond. I don't know if he got annoyed or angry, but he stood up really fast and I panicked," she whispers.

"It's alright. It's over now and you're safe in my room," I say, rocking back and forth.

She nods her head, lets go of me, and gets comfortable on my bed.

"It's so soft," she whispers, running her hand over the bed.

I let out a little chuckle and nod my head. My mattress is really soft, and I had honestly forgotten what it feels like to sleep on it. I don't know if I will be able to sleep on it after sleeping on the hard concrete for over two months.

I watch as she slowly starts to fall asleep. She looks so peaceful laying on my bed. I wonder if she ever got to sleep on a bed while she was kidnapped. We never got around to talking about that, and I honestly want to know now.

I lay right next to Estella and try to get comfortable. I toss and turn for several minutes, not getting comfortable with so many thoughts running through my head. I always remember falling asleep with one of Noah's shirts on, his smell always puts me to sleep fast. Would it still work?

I carefully get out of bed and walk towards the door. I stop and think this through. Should I be doing this? What if he catches me and gets angry?

I take a deep breath in and push those thoughts away. I peek my head outside and look around. I can hear Butch and Noah's voices downstairs. I quietly leave the room and head towards his.

Opening the door, I fully step in and take a breath. It smells like him, and I can feel my body start to relax some. I look around the room and realize nothing has changed in here, but his bed looks even more tempting than it did before. Maybe I could just take a short nap before he comes up to sleep. I don't think he would mind if I did. What he doesn't know won't kill him.

I quickly make my way towards his bed, pulling the covers back and getting in. I bring the covers all the way to my chin and inhale his scent. My eyes start to droop closed and I find it harder and harder to stay awake, so I don't fight it anymore and fall asleep.

CHAPTER TWENTY-FIVE

MARCY

TWO MONTHS LATER

Things around here have almost gone back to normal. Oliver and Michael have been home for a couple of weeks now, and it's been so hectic. It feels like every thirty minutes they are screaming and crying. It's driving me insane, and I think it's making the guys mad.

Thankfully, my room is soundproof, so I don't hear my twin brothers waking up every couple of hours. I have always been a light sleeper, so my dad soundproofed my room so I wouldn't wake up when the guys did stuff in the middle of the night. They also wanted to not hear me scream and yell when I was playing.

I think the guys in the MC have asked my parents if they can find a house to live in. They all look tired. Everyone is grouchy and I don't know how much more everyone can take of their screaming. Some of the guys have asked me and Estella why we look so tired, since they know my room is soundproof. I just brush it off and say I leave the door cracked and can hear everything.

I'm grateful to have the room be soundproofed now, because I don't wake up everyone with my nightmares. I make sure my room is locked now while Estella and I sleep at night. One time Noah came in and heard me screaming.

I completely shut him out from it. I told him I was okay and that it was a nightmare from when I was a kid. He knew I was lying, but I'm not ready to talk about it yet. I don't know if I will ever be ready. He hasn't pushed me much to talk about it, but he has cornered me several times and asked me to open up.

Estella and I wake up every night from the nightmares. Our minds know we have escaped from that nightmare, but now it's torturing us with this nightmare.

The night I snuck into Noah's room and fell asleep, he brought me back to my room. I'm grateful because I woke up that night from a nightmare and then woke up again for Estella. He told me that morning he didn't want to bring me back, but he knew my dad would have a fit if he found us in the same room.

I've gotten better around everyone, and so has Estella. We have managed to look into everyone's eyes, but if they start yelling, we revert back to our old selves. We normally keep to ourselves, but if people talk to us, we do engage some. It's definitely been hard, but everyone has been patient with us so far.

My parents have tried to get Estella and me to talk about what happened, but we haven't told them anything. I don't know if we will ever be able to tell them anything. I know it's not good, to bottle things up, but I know if they found out what happened, that all hell would break loose.

Noah has put together some stuff from my one nightmare, but he hasn't even scratched the surface. He's definitely pushed me more to talk about it, but every time he brings it up, I come up with an excuse. I'm starting to run out of excuses now.

Estella has gotten better about being around the girls, but any guy she completely shuts down. Butch has tried to get to know her more and she can look into his eyes for a while, but if he moves too fast or even slightly raises his voice, she shuts down and runs away.

I've had to push my emotions even more aside and pretend that I'm okay. That nothing is wrong and I'm their daughter again. I've fooled everyone but my parents, Butch, Noah, and Gears. I smile and laugh when people tell jokes, but it's all fake.

I've gotten more comfortable with Noah and him touching me, but sometimes I do flinch if I'm not paying attention to him. I can see the regret and anger in his eyes when I do. It breaks my heart, but at the same time I don't want him to know what happened. He'll definitely not want me then.

Right now, I'm getting ready for a barbeque that we are having to celebrate the twins, Estella, Dom, and I coming home. They wanted to wait until now so all of us could have a chance to get things back to normal. To feel like a part of the family again.

I know Estella and I don't feel like a part of the family, especially Estella. She doesn't know anyone really, besides me. She doesn't know how to interact with people. I've been trying to help, but it's hard when I don't even want to interact with these people.

"Do you think it will get easier?" Estella whispers.

I look over at her and watch as she's looking out the window. Her body language is relaxed, but I know she's uncomfortable. She's hugging herself like she doesn't know what to do or how to act. I've asked her if she wants to find her family, but she just shakes her head.

"Maybe. I don't really know," I reply. "We'll figure it out together."

"I hope it does," she says.

"Me too."

Maybe I should talk to someone about what happened, but I don't know who. I don't want to tell anyone here in fear that they will use it against me or never be able to look at me the same. They already look at us like we are different, and I don't like it one bit.

"Living here is so strange. Everyone is nice. Too nice," she says, looking at me.

I chuckle and nod my head. "Yes, they are. It's weird, isn't it?"

She nods her head and looks back out the window. She's been looking out that window for half an hour, analyzing the people in the backyard. I don't blame her, I would too if I didn't know everyone.

"Ready?" I ask Estella.

She nods her head and grabs my hand. I gently squeeze it as we walk out of my room, down the stairs, and outside to the backyard. The backyard is packed with people from the MC. Their families are here. Kids are running, screaming, and enjoying themselves.

All eyes turn towards us when we step out on the porch, making us both freeze. My heart starts beating faster as they continue to stare. Estella squeezes my hand even tighter, and it takes everything in me to not turn around and run.

"Marcy! Estella! Come see your brothers," my mom says.

Since day one of being back, my mom has accepted Estella as part of our family. Estella asked me a couple nights after first arriving if she was serious and I said yes. She was definitely shocked and didn't know how to act. She still doesn't.

Estella and I walk towards my parents where Gears and

Butch are holding my baby brothers. I honestly don't know how to feel about my parents having a kid when I'm almost an adult. It's weird, but my parents seem happy, so I leave it alone. It does hurt that they are giving them more attention and not their daughter who was gone for two months, but at the same time I'm grateful because I don't know what I would have done with all that attention.

"Here, you can hold him," Butch says.

He goes towards Estella, and I watch as she flinches when he moves too fast. He either didn't notice or is pretending like he didn't see it. I'm guessing he is pretending because it was a big flinch. He passes the baby off to Estella and I have to hold my laugh in. She honestly doesn't know what to do with babies, but I'm the same way. She looks awkward holding Oliver.

Gears passes Michael to me, and I try my best to not look awkward. I look down at Michael and can't help but feel jealous that he's a baby and I'm not. He doesn't have to worry about anything. Everything is done for him.

I look up and catch my parents looking at Estella and me, wide smiles spread across their faces. My mom comes forward and kisses our foreheads.

"I'm so proud of you two," she whispers to us.

Proud of what? Proud of faking everything? I don't think that's something you should be proud of.

I take in a deep breath as I feel my arms start to ache. I'm still not used to holding heavy things in my arms. I haven't gained all the weight that I've lost. Butch has been making Estella and I eat every couple of hours. He wants us to get healthier again.

I think Butch is doing it for two reasons. One for us to get healthier, but the second reason is to be close to Estella. He's taken an interest in her. It's weird, but he's so patient with her.

He tries to make her comfortable and asks her all types of questions about what she likes and doesn't like.

I'm a little concerned about him taking a liking towards her. I don't know if this is what she needs right now, but maybe it is. I've been keeping a close eye on them in case anything happens. They are never alone. Estella won't go anywhere without me, and I don't blame her. We stick together, right now.

"Here, let me take them. I bet your arms are getting tired," my dad says, reaching for Oliver and Michael.

Estella and I both flinch as he moves too fast. He gives us a smile and grabs the twins. I hear Estella let out a little sigh of content when Oliver is out of her arms, and it makes me smile a little bit.

"Why don't you guys go talk to some people," my mom suggests.

Estella and I freeze at her words. Butch gives my mom a concerned look. We haven't ever started a conversation with anyone since we got here. Everyone has approached us and that's how I like it. Well, I would like it if no one talked to us, but I can't have it all my way.

Estella grabs my hand with her shaky one and squeezes it. How do I get out of this without sounding rude?

"I'll go with them," Butch says.

Not much better, but maybe he can just do the talking.

"You're needed cooking," my mom says.

It looks like luck is not on our side. Maybe I can say I need to go to the bathroom. No, that won't work because we just came out here. My mom will not like that we are trying to leave.

"It's only making the salads. The meat is all done," Butch says.

My mom narrows her eyes at him, but he doesn't back down. Before she can say anything, I feel arms wrap around my waist and I let out a little scream as I jump. I stare with wide eyes at Noah who is holding his hands up.

Estella wraps her arms around me and brings me in closer to her. Everyone knows not to touch us without us being able to see them. I look around and realize everyone is staring at us and I bow my head. I hate that everyone is looking at us.

"Nothing to see. Go back to your conversations!" Butch yells.

I can slowly hear conversations start back up, but it's not as loud as it was before. I look up and make eye contact with Noah.

"I'm sorry," I whisper.

I know I don't have to apologize, but I just want people to know I don't mean it.

"You caught me off guard," I speak again.

"It's okay. I should have known not to do that. You were just doing so well the past couple of days," he says.

I flinch at his words. I've been pretending more and more. Holding my breath when people come near me. Doing everything I can to not flinch when they touch me.

"I shouldn't have screamed and moved. I know I'm not in any danger here," I reply.

"You don't have to explain yourself. You're okay," Butch says.

I shake my head and wrap my arms around Estella.

"How about you guys sit down and relax? We'll bring some food to you when it's ready," my dad says.

I nod my head and lead Estella and me to some empty chairs. No one is around us and I can feel ourselves starting to relax some.

"Maybe it won't get better," I whisper. "Maybe we should leave. Go to a cabin in a forest and live in peace."

"That sounds like a wonderful idea," she says.

"Give us a chance. It will get better. I promise," Butch says out of nowhere.

I stare at him with wide eyes. I didn't think anyone was close to us. I take in his form and realize he's holding two plates in his hands.

"Don't tell anyone," I plead.

"I won't as long as you won't leave and give everyone a chance," he replies.

I nod my head.

"Words," he says. "From both of you."

"I promise," we both respond.

"Good. Now, here are your plates of food. I expect half of it to be gone."

We nod our heads and slowly start to eat. He sits down in front of us and watches everyone around us.

"It gets better. Let some people in and tell them what all happened. It's hard, but it will get easier," Butch says out of nowhere.

He isn't looking at us, but we know he's speaking to us.

"Just try. That's all I'm asking," he says.

"Okay," I respond.

Estella and I end up eating half of our plates before we get full. Butch seems pretty satisfied with it. Noah came and sat down a few minutes before, but hasn't said anything to us. He's only talked to Butch. Maybe it won't be bad after all. Maybe I could talk to someone here. Maybe Butch. He seems to understand a lot more than anyone else around here.

EPILOGUE

MARCY

"Hey, Marcy. What are you doing?" Noah asks, wrapping his arm around my waist.

I hold in my flinch, not wanting him to suspect anything. I've done great the past couple of days. Ever since the barbecue, I've been trying my best not to flinch around Noah.

"Just watching my parents take care of Oliver and Michael," I reply, leaning into his touch.

"They are doing pretty good with them, don't you think?" he asks.

"Yeah, they are. Everyone else is great with them, too."

He lets out a content sigh and starts moving his thumbs in a circular motion on my hips. He's done this the past couple of days to try to get me to relax into him more. I just force myself to relax but still be on high alert.

It's my fault for misleading him on that. I forced myself to relax the first time and I guess he thought he really helped me. I don't have the heart to tell him that he hasn't. He would ask too many questions if he knew.

He's still asking me questions every day to try and get me to open up. I just tell him I'm fine and try to move on.

I'm waiting for the day he explodes and tells me I'm not okay. My body and mind are anticipating it. I can feel myself starting to be more alert and keeping my guard up more.

My parents think everything is fine now. I apologized and told them that it was so abnormal for me to do it. That I had been so good for a while. I lied and told them that I've been writing things out and getting through it all. They told me everything was okay and that they can see a difference in me.

That they are proud of me for coming so far.

That broke my heart. If only they knew what was really happening. Everyone else believes that I've gotten better, besides Noah.

I can see it in his eyes that he doesn't believe anything I've said. He has the same look he gave me before I got kidnapped. It breaks my heart to be lying to him and knowing he doesn't believe me. I may break soon and just spill my guts to him.

I bet Butch doesn't believe I've gotten better, either. He's been keeping a close eye on Estella and me. More so Estella than me, but he still knows. He says little things like 'it's okay' or 'it's going to get better' but I don't know if it ever will.

Estella has asked me about Butch. She's curious about him. I've told her that he has taken a liking to her, but she just shakes her head. She's tried to block him out, but he won't allow her to.

He's always making sure she is okay and that she has everything she needs or wants. He went out and got a couple pairs of clothes for her so she would have something of her own. Let's just say it didn't end very well.

Estella completely shut down and asked him if he wanted her body as a tradeoff. Thankfully, no one was there besides Noah and me. Butch told her that he wasn't expecting anything and didn't want anything. That he just wanted her to be happy.

She didn't understand what he meant. Why did he want her happy when he didn't even know her? I know Butch is going to sit her down at some point and tell her. I'm waiting for him to ask me if he can talk to her alone.

"You're great with them," he says, bringing me closer to his body.

"I'm not. I don't know how to act around them," I reply.

"You do amazing. You don't have to act around them. They are babies. Just hold, feed, and talk to them."

I wish it was that simple. They normally cry in my arms and no matter what I do, they won't calm down.

"They cry a lot," I say.

"They are babies. They are always going to cry at some point," he chuckles.

He does have a point, but they don't cry in Butch, Noah, or Gear's arms. It hurts, but I'm trying not to think about it too much.

"How about we go sit outside and talk?" Noah suggests.

"Sure," I reply.

With his arms still wrapped around me, we walk out of the living room and into the backyard. We sit down on one of the chairs and I snuggle into his arms.

"Tell me a story?" I ask.

I haven't asked him in a long time to tell me a story. He's pretty good at telling stories and at one moment before getting kidnapped I was excited about our future. He does so well with kids and his stories suck you in.

"Okay, give me a second to think about one," he replies.

I stare off into the distance, waiting for him to talk. I know I should be calm and relaxed, but I can't. My body is on alert. I feel myself starting to crumble the longer we sit here. How much longer can I go like this? Pretending that everything is okay?

"I love you," he whispers, kissing the side of my head.

I stay silent. My whole mind is blank from shock. Those

words break me more than I could ever imagine. How can he love someone that is so damaged like me? That won't talk to him and tell him the things that happened to me?

"We are going to get through this. I'm with you every step of the way. You can push me away. I'm just going to chase right after you," he says. "I'm never leaving you. No matter what you do, I'm not leaving."

Tears appear in my eyes, and I blink several times, trying to get them away. What he doesn't know is that those words are about to break me. I know I should be happy that he wants me. I know that he should be my happily ever after. But I just can't believe him after all that I went through. Maybe he will be my happily ever after, but I just don't know how to process it. It's all too much.

ACKNOWLEDGMENTS

Thank you to everyone who has taken the time to read this book! It means a lot to me.

I want to say thank you to my beta readers. Thank you for pointing things out and pushing me to be a better writer!

I want to thank my ARC readers! I wouldn't have been able to do this without you guys!

Thank you to my cover artist, Ever After Cover Design, for doing an amazing job on this cover! I absolutely love this cover!

ABOUT THE AUTHOR

C.E. Kingsley is a spicy romance author. She loves to read and take pictures in her spare time. She is in her senior year at college studying digital marketing and advertising.

Want to get early access to cover reveals, spicy scenes, chapters, merch, and more?

Join my Pattern: https://www.patreon.com/user?u=74839459

Want to get notified when she has another book coming out? Follow her on Facebook, Instagram, Goodreads, TikTok, Patreon, and sign up for her Newsletter.

NEWSLETTER:

FACEBOOK: Kingsley's Coven of Spicy Readers (Group)

INSTAGRAM: @authorc.ekingsley

GOODREADS: Author C.E. Kingsley

TIKTOK: @authorc.ekingsley

ALSO BY C.E. KINGSLEY

Hell's Reaper MC Series

Behind the Burns (Book 1)

Behind the Scheme (Book 2)

Standalone

Dante's Little Dancer (novella)

Coming Soon

The Love Fountain Series (Monster Romance)

The Dragon's Sanctuary (Coming 10/22)

Made in the USA
Las Vegas, NV
31 August 2022

54453641R00122